JOHNNY BOO MEETS DRAGON PUNCHER!

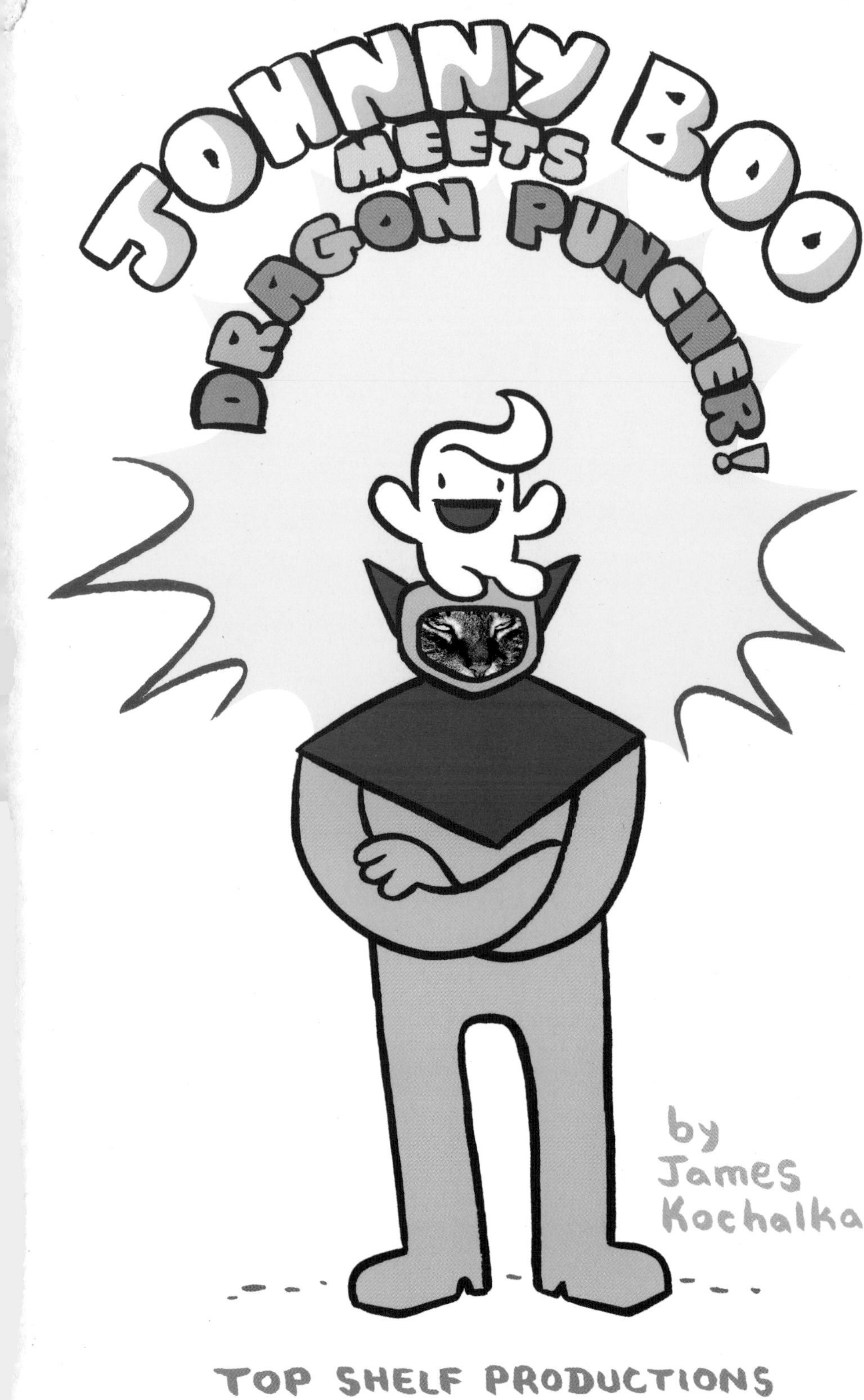

by
James
Kochalka

TOP SHELF PRODUCTIONS
MARIETTA, GA

IN LOVING MEMORY OF

SPANDY

1994 – 2014

~WE MISS YOU~

Johnny Boo Meets Dragon Puncher © 2015 James Kochalka.

Published by Top Shelf Productions, PO Box 1282, Marietta, GA 30061-1282, USA. Editor-in-Chief: Chris Staros. Top Shelf Productions is an imprint of IDW Publishing, a division of Idea and Design Works, LLC. Offices: 5080 Santa Fe Street, San Diego, CA 92109. Top Shelf Productions®, the Top Shelf logo, Idea and Design Works®, and the IDW logo are registered trademarks of Idea and Design Works, LLC. All Rights Reserved. With the exception of small excerpts of artwork used for review purposes, none of the contents of this publication may be reprinted without the permission of IDW Publishing. IDW Publishing does not read or accept unsolicited submissions of ideas, stories, or artwork.

Edited by Leigh Walton.

Visit our online catalog at www.topshelfcomix.com.

Printed in Korea.

ISBN 978-1-60309-368-2

18   17   16   15   5   4   3   2   1

CHAPTER ONE

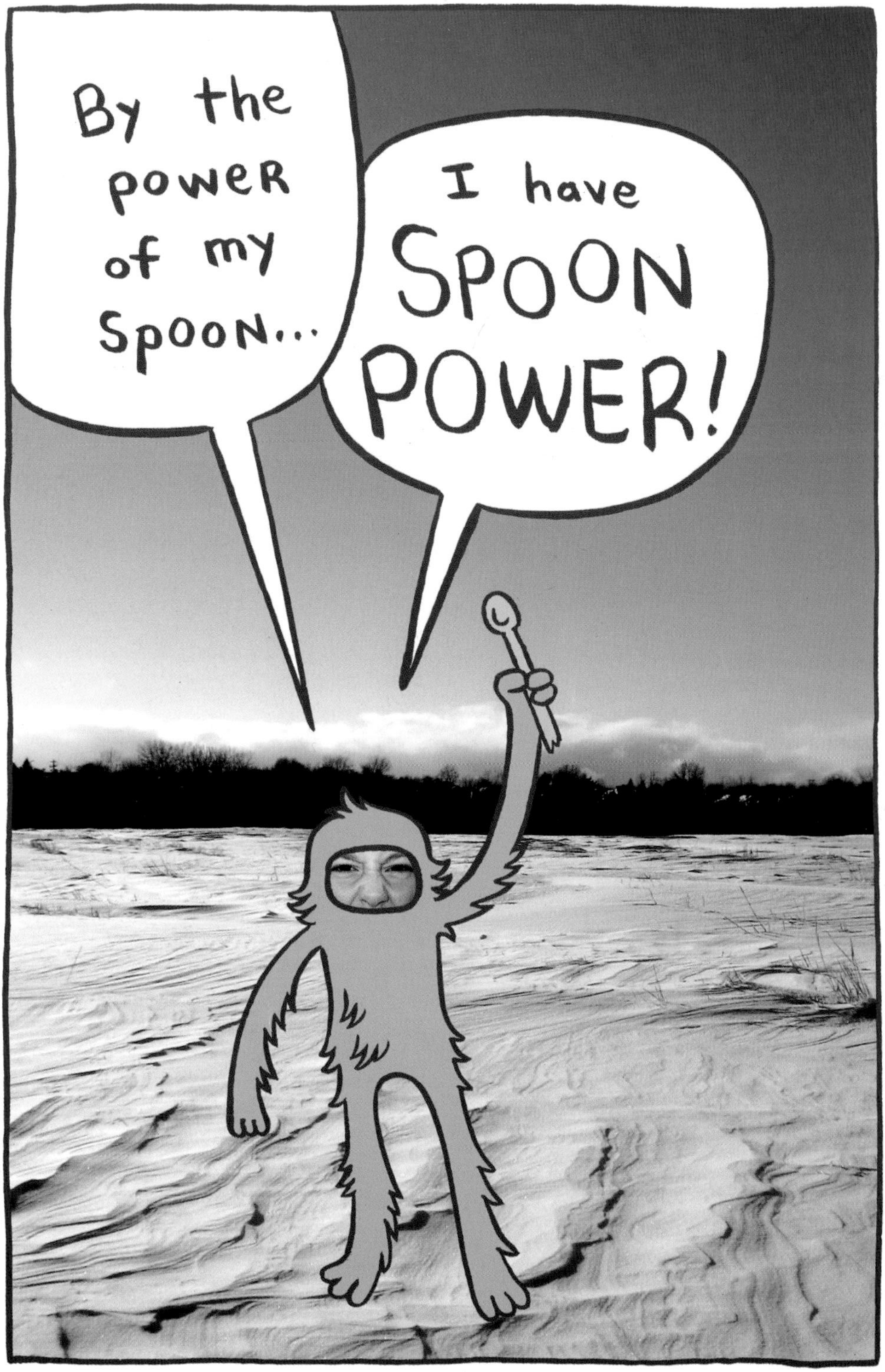
By the power of my spoon...
I have SPOON POWER!

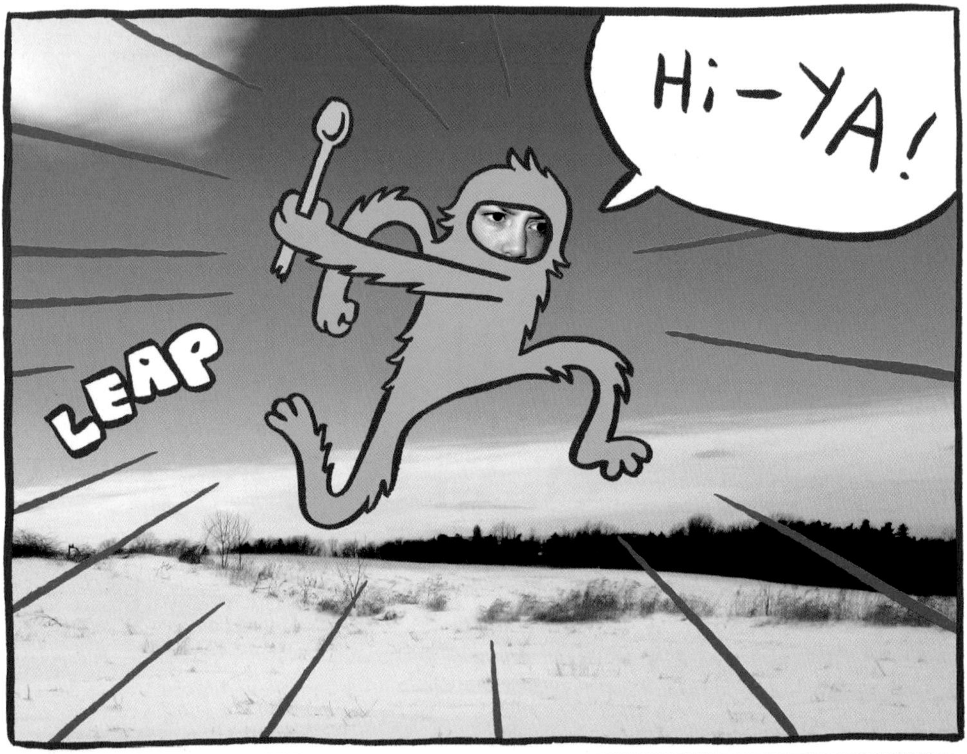
HI-YA!
LEAP

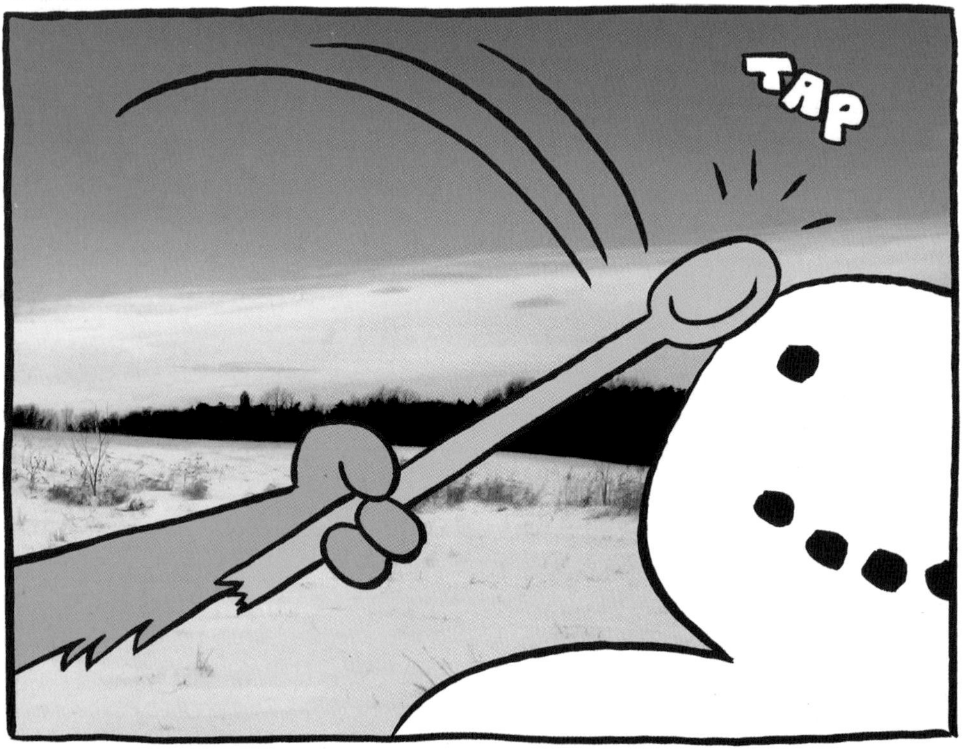
TAP

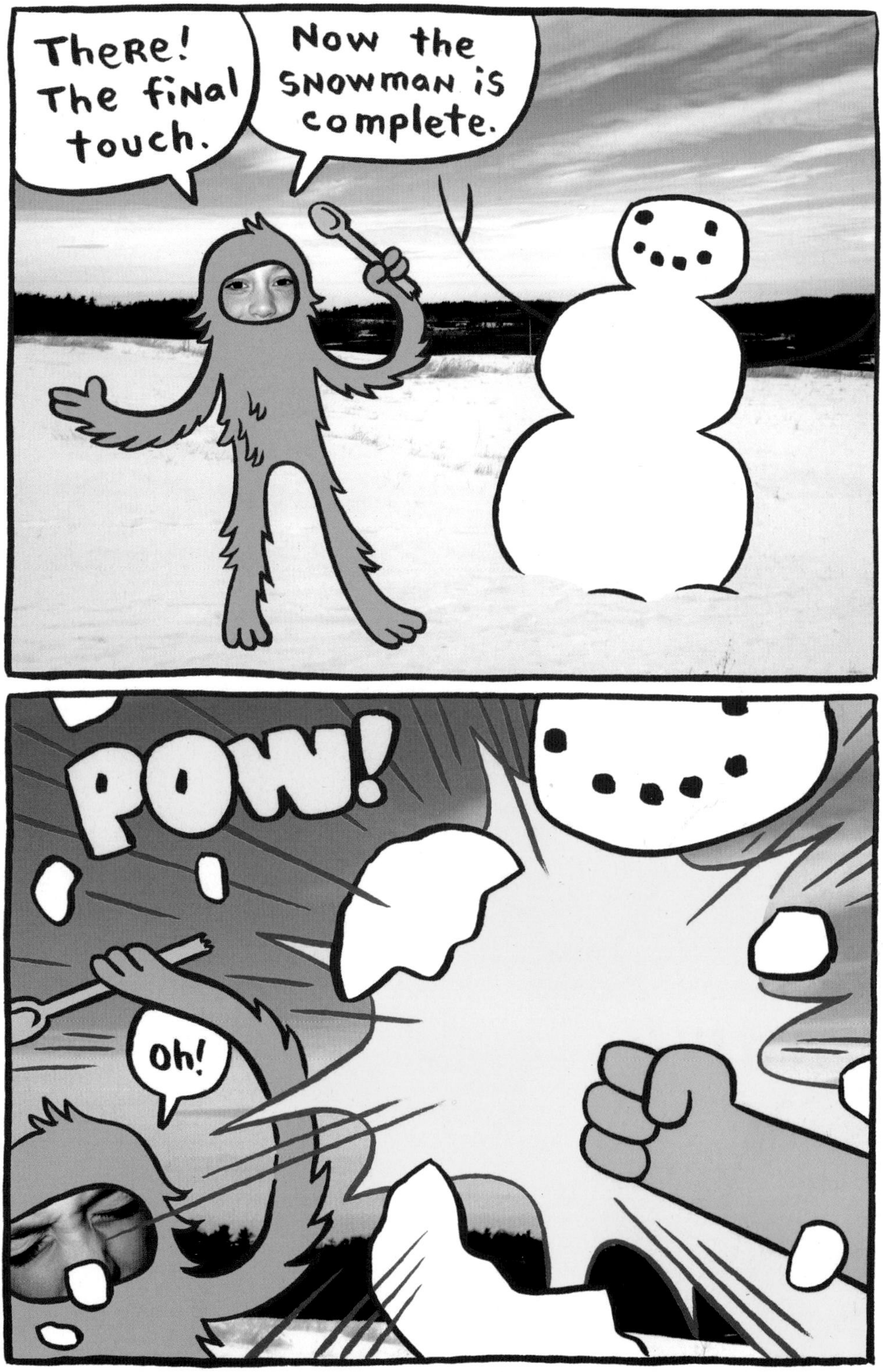
There! The final touch.
Now the snowman is complete.
POW!
Oh!

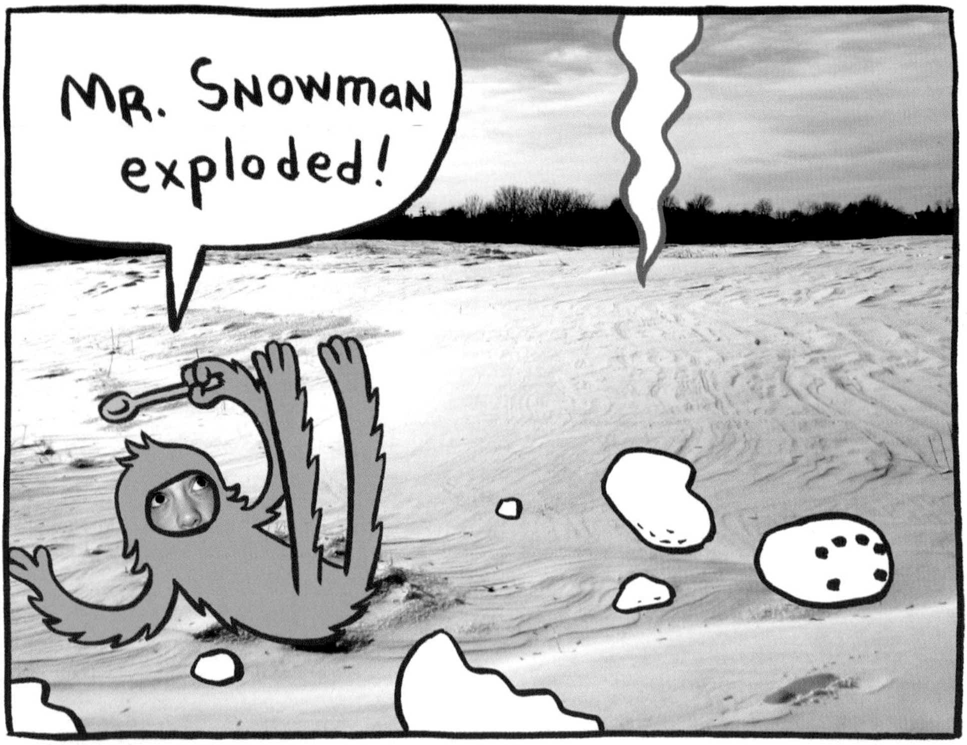
Mr. Snowman exploded!

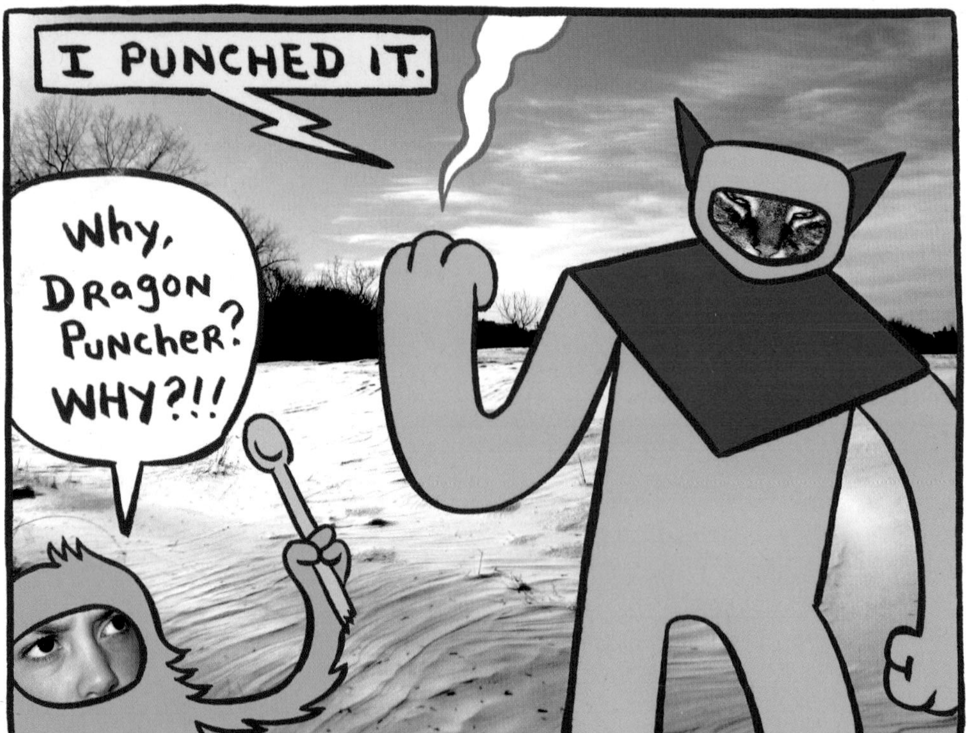
I PUNCHED IT.
Why, Dragon Puncher? WHY?!!

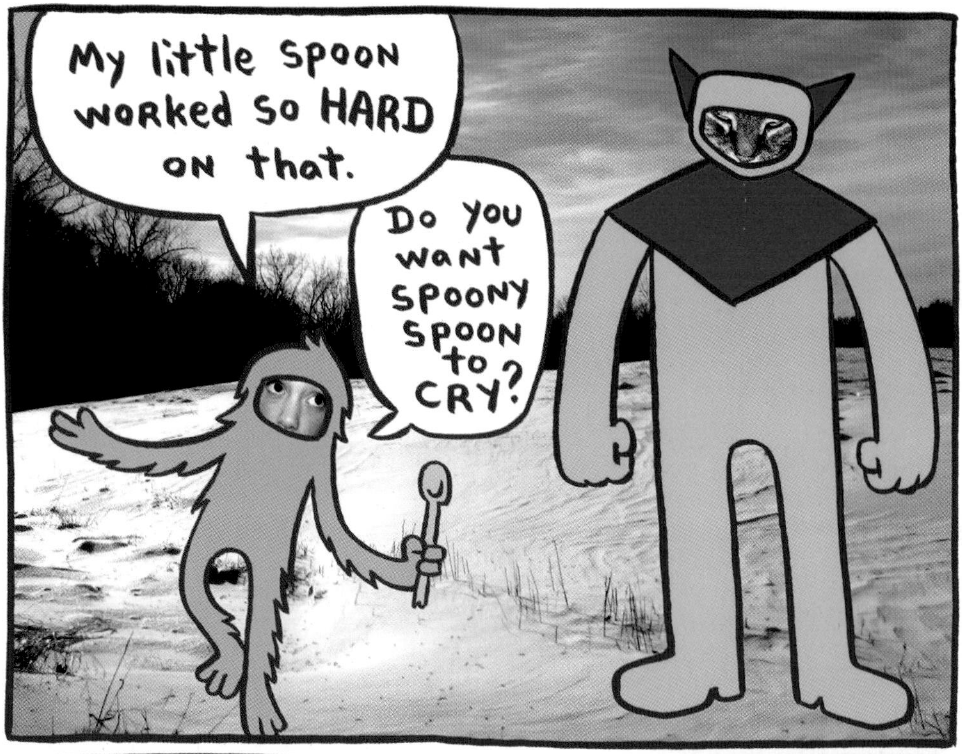
My little spoon worked so HARD on that.
Do you want spoony spoon to CRY?

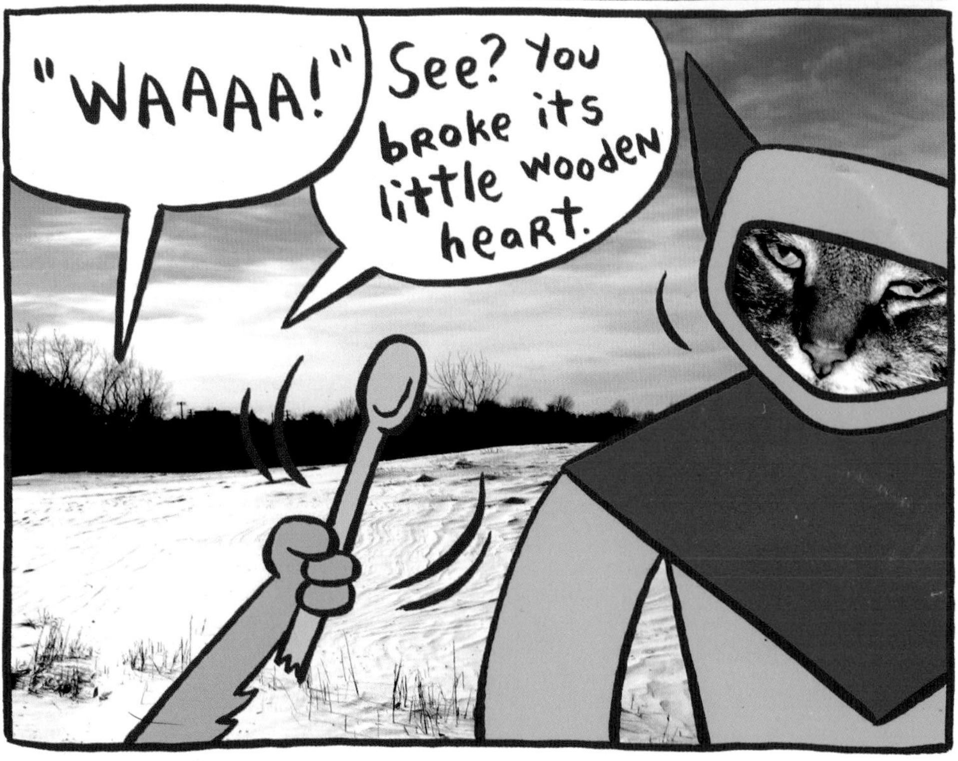
"WAAAA!"
See? You broke its little wooden heart.

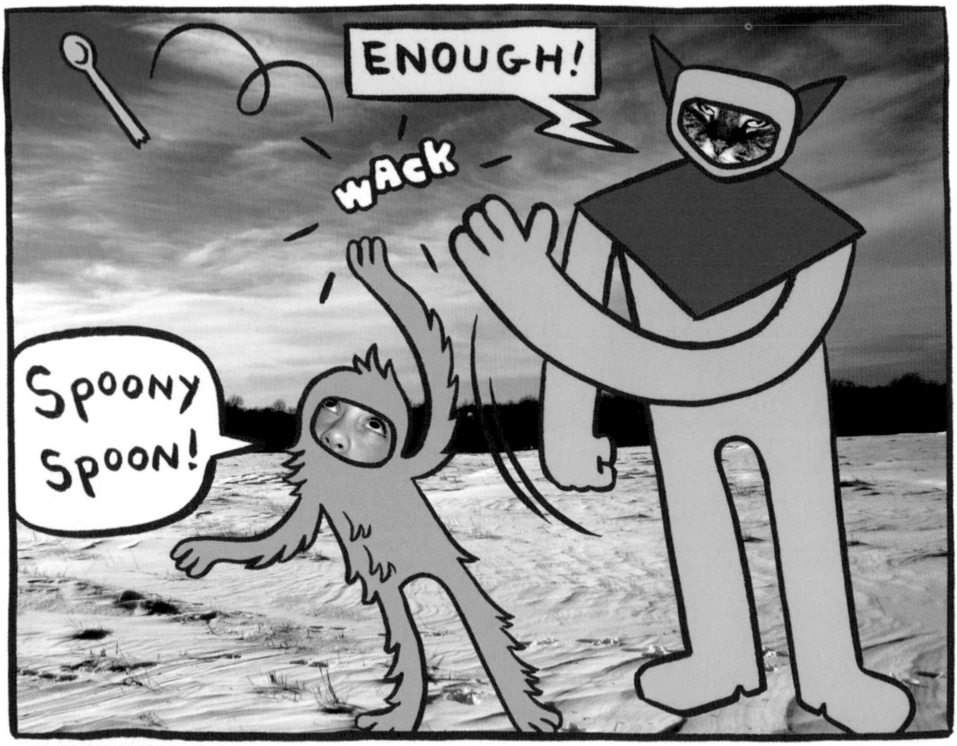
ENOUGH!
WACK
Spoony Spoon!

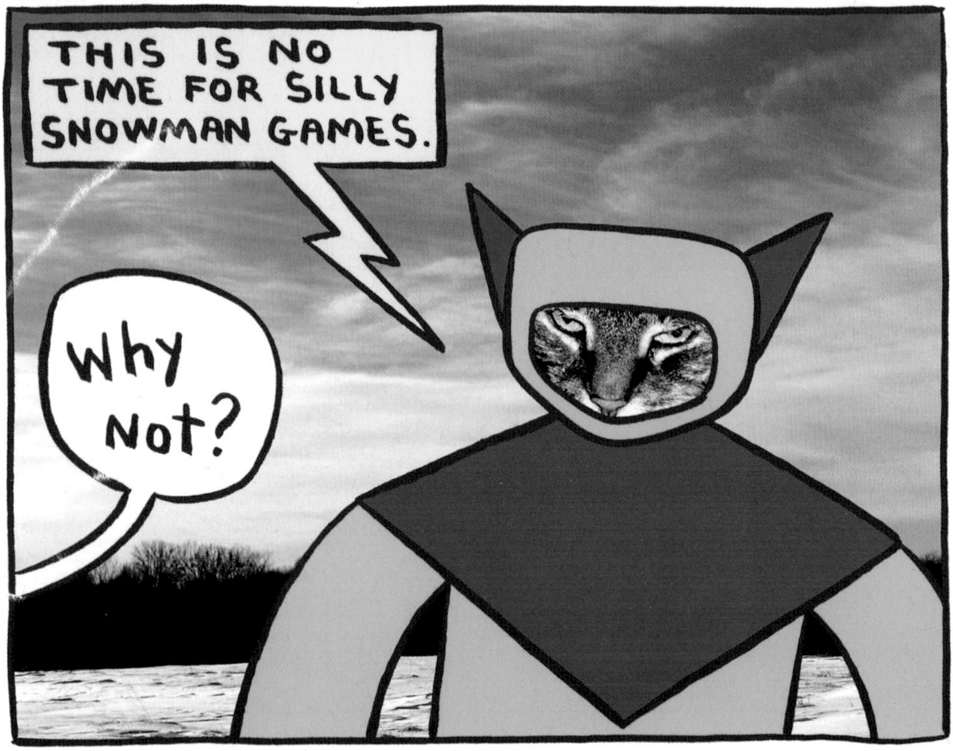
THIS IS NO TIME FOR SILLY SNOWMAN GAMES.
Why Not?

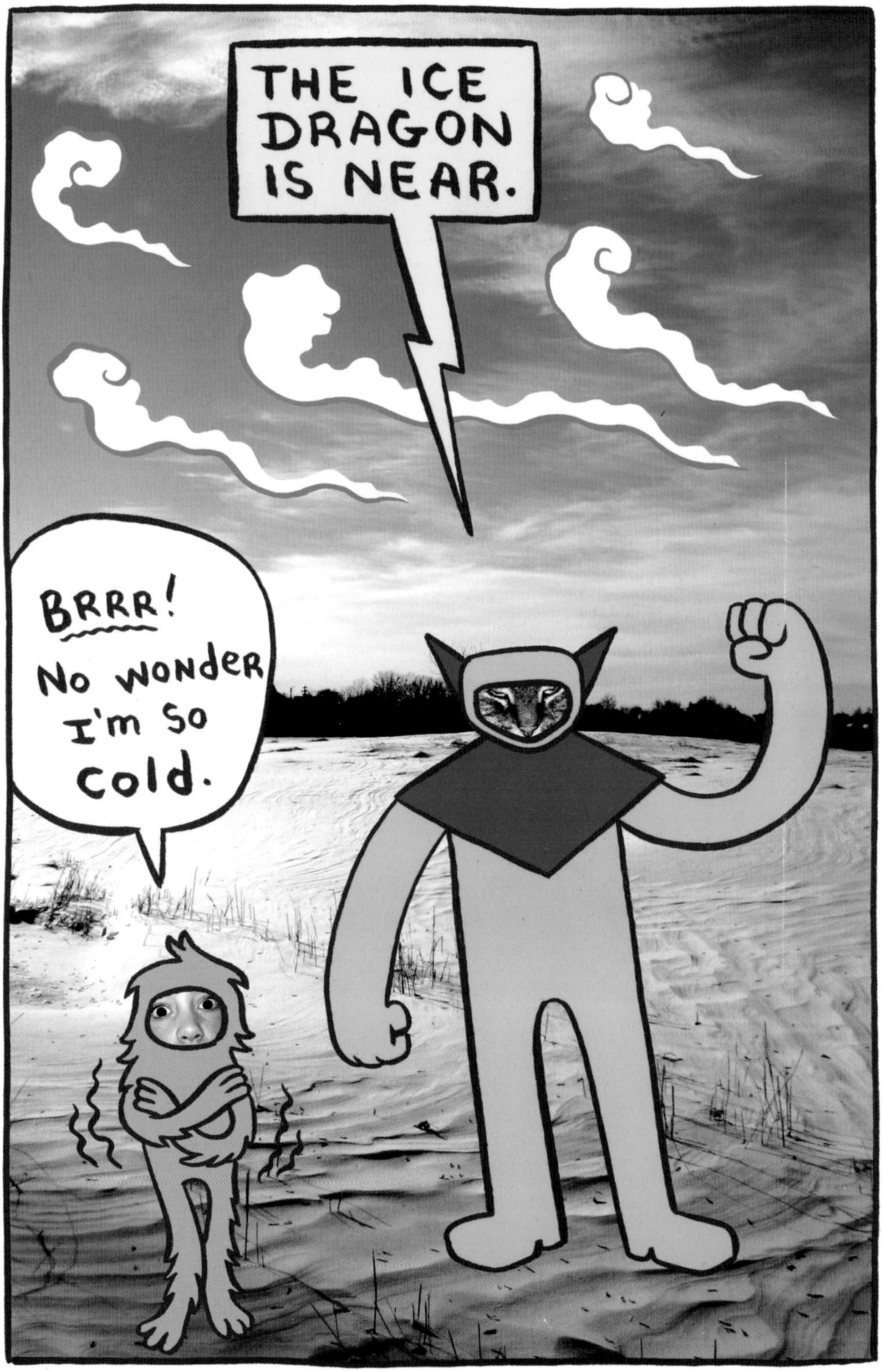
THE ICE DRAGON IS NEAR.
BRRR! No wonder I'm so cold.

CHAPTER TWO:

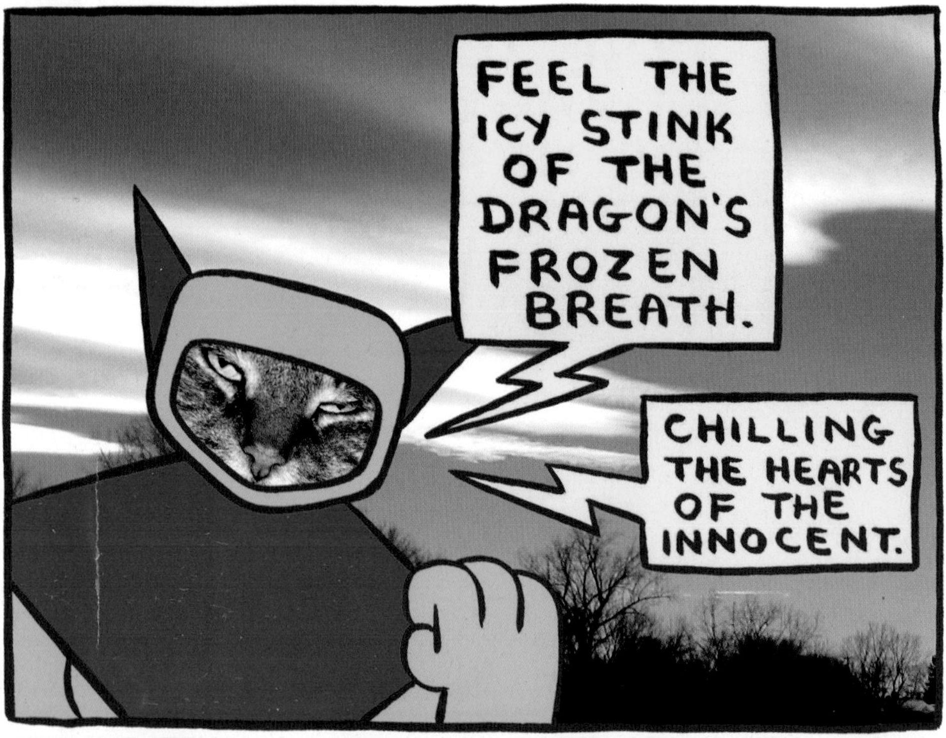
FEEL THE ICY STINK OF THE DRAGON'S FROZEN BREATH.
CHILLING THE HEARTS OF THE INNOCENT.

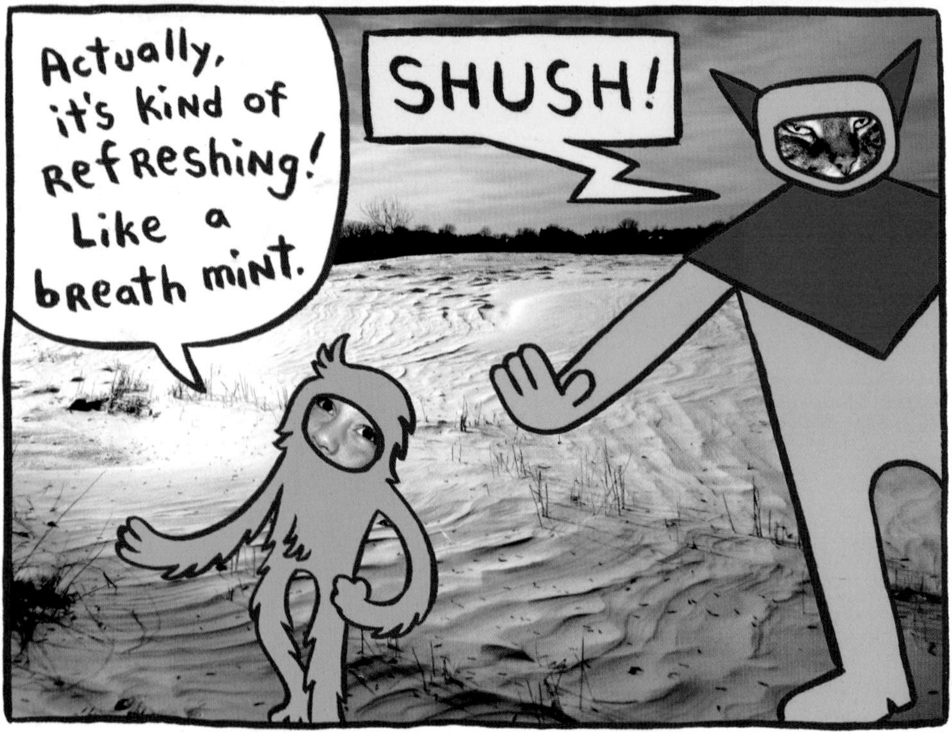
Actually, it's kind of refreshing! Like a breath mint.
SHUSH!

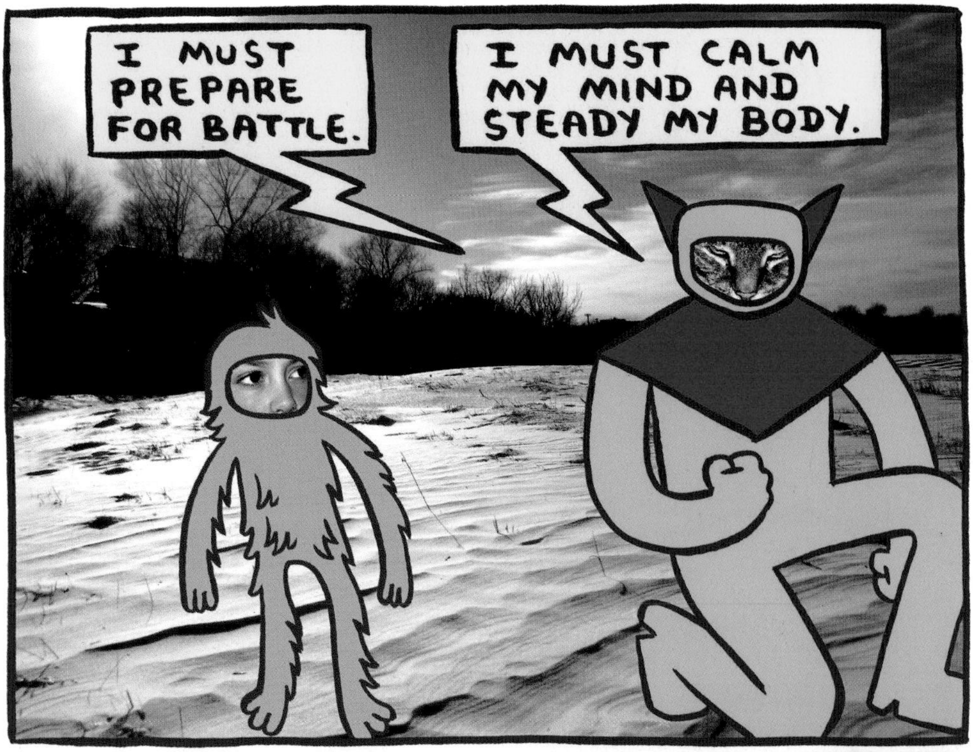
I MUST PREPARE FOR BATTLE.
I MUST CALM MY MIND AND STEADY MY BODY.

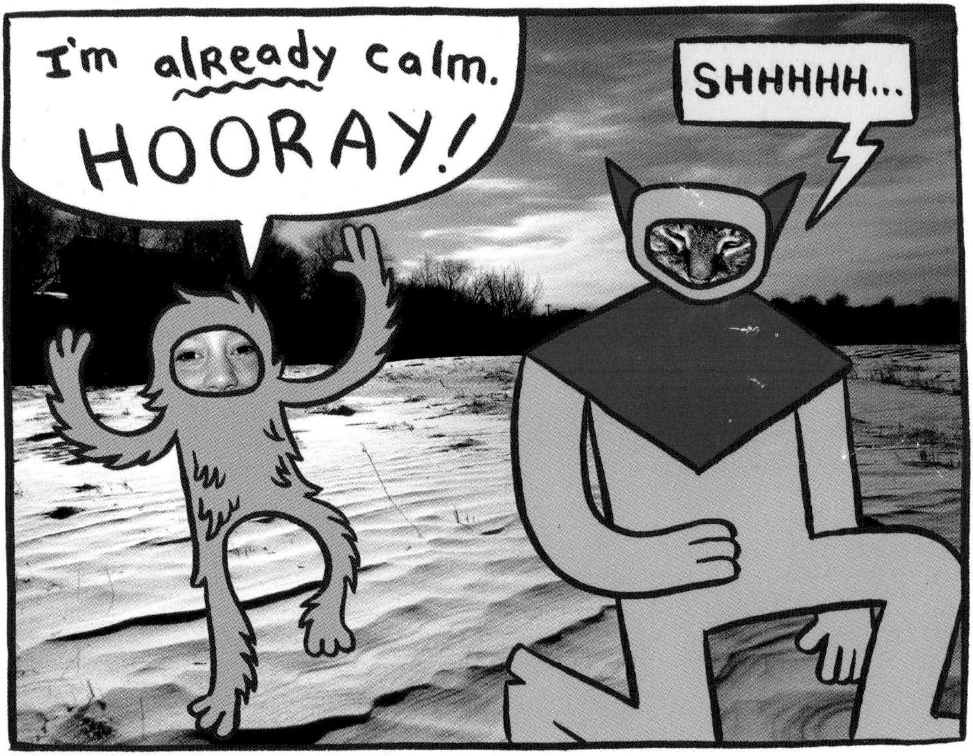
I'm already calm. HOORAY!
SHHHHH...

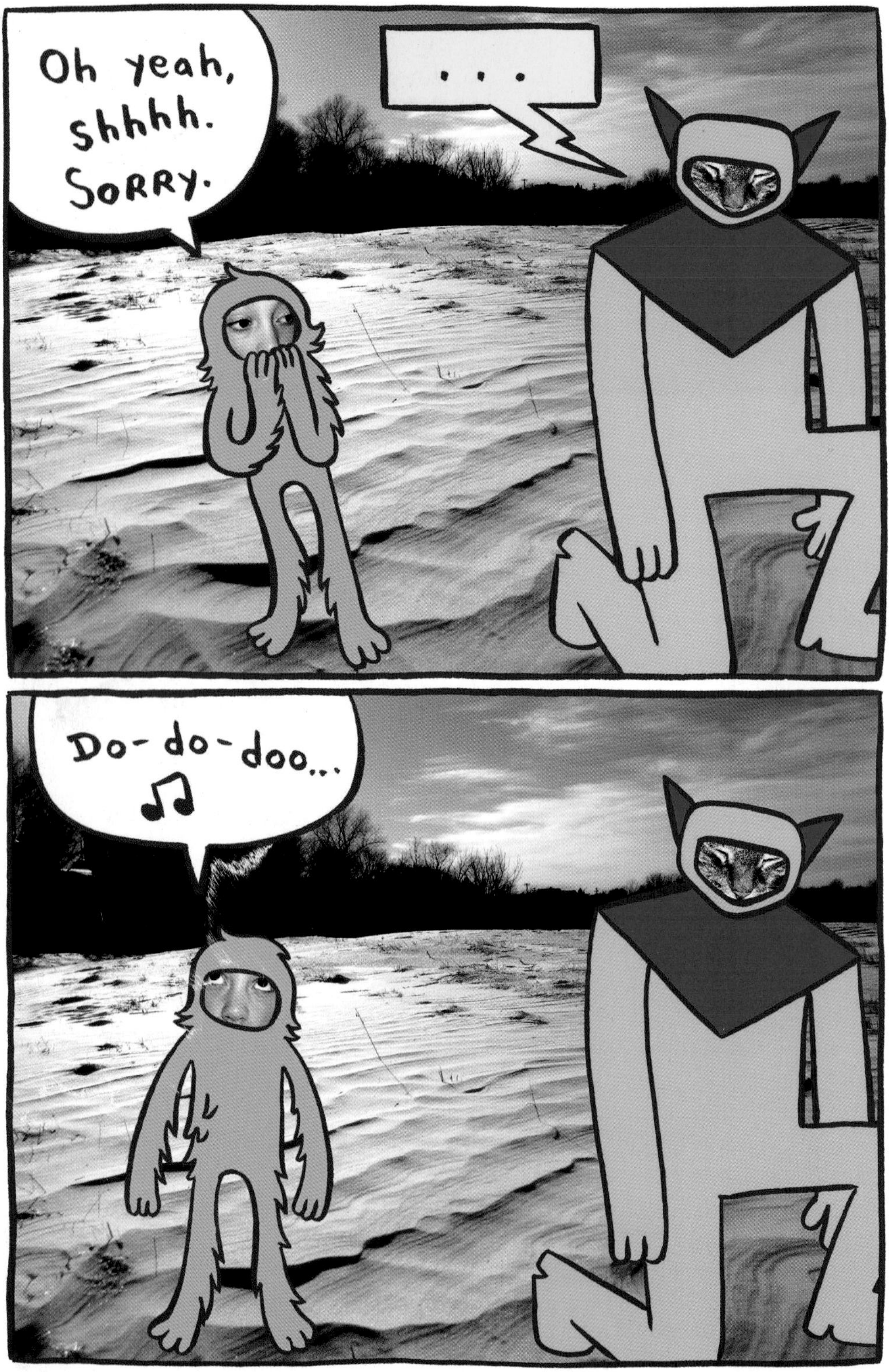
Oh yeah, shhhh. SORRY.
. . .
Do-do-doo...

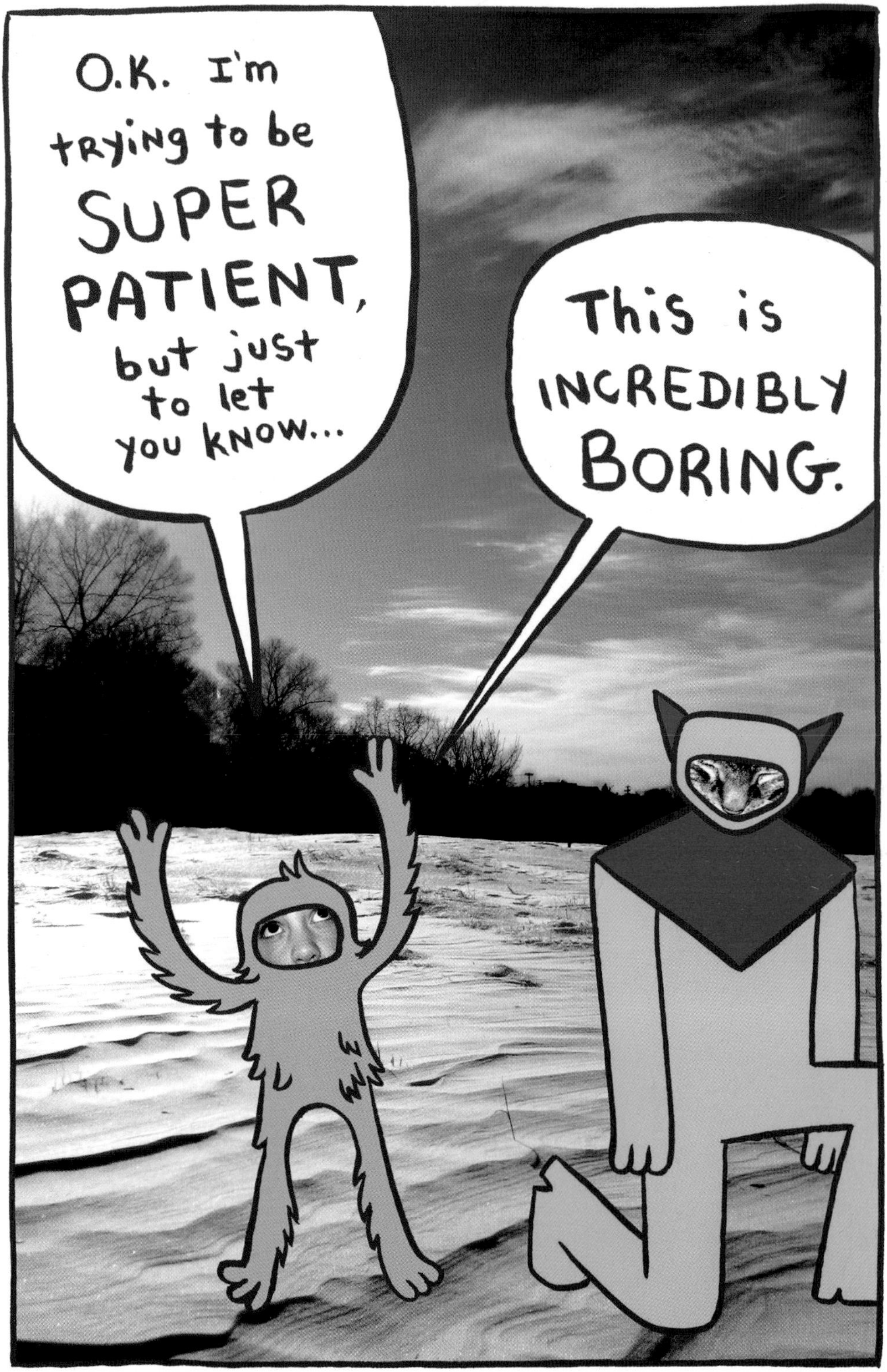
O.K. I'm trying to be SUPER PATIENT, but just to let you know...
This is INCREDIBLY BORING.

CHAPTER THREE:

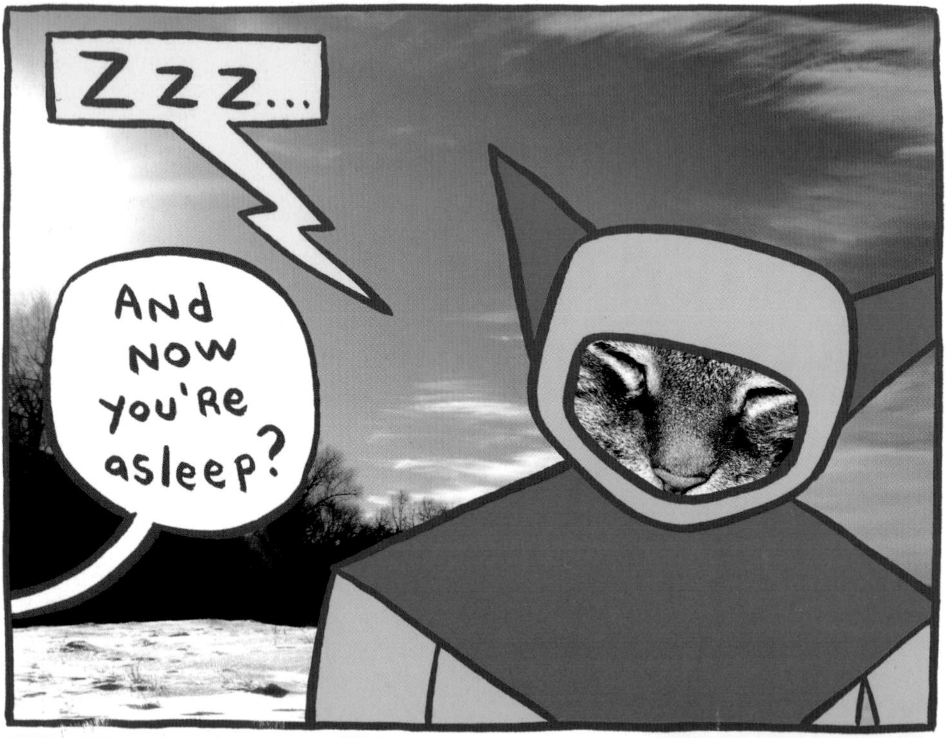
Zzz...
And now you're asleep?

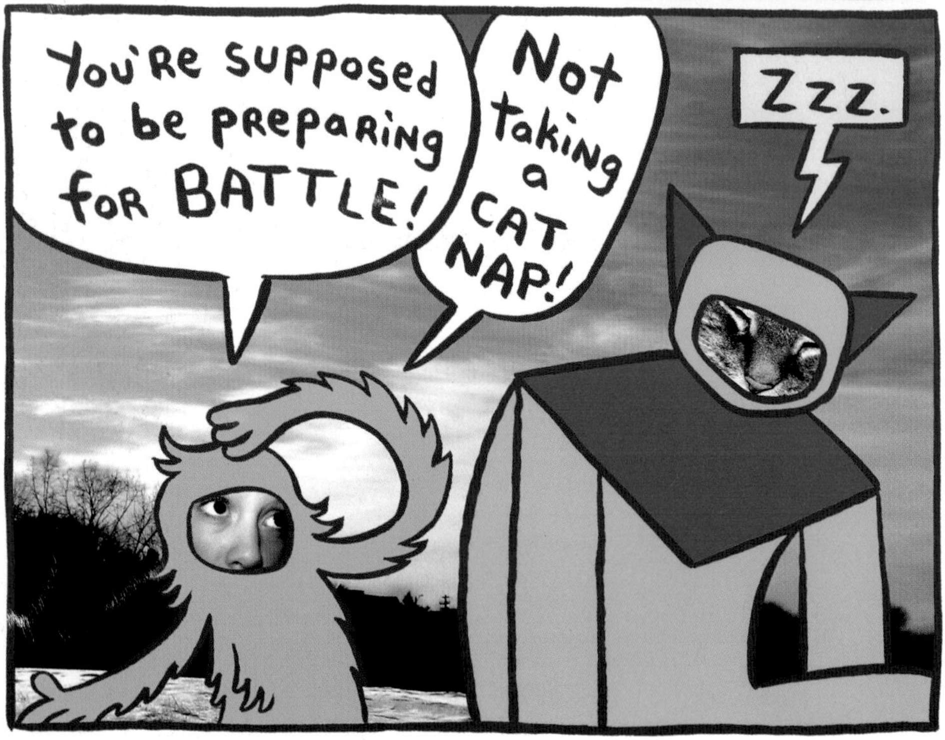
You're supposed to be preparing for BATTLE!
Not taking a CAT NAP!
Zzz.

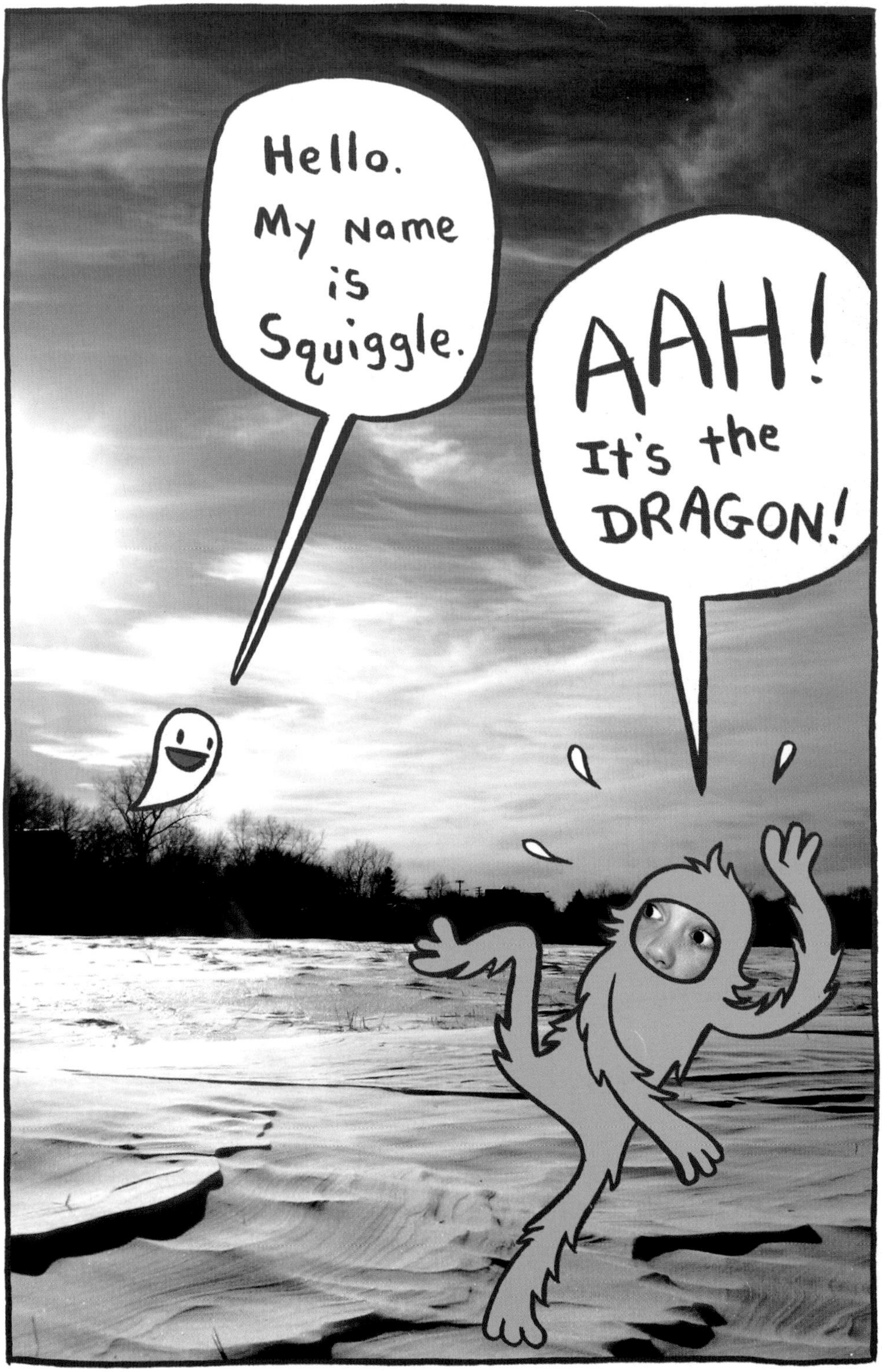
Hello. My name is Squiggle.
AAH! It's the DRAGON!

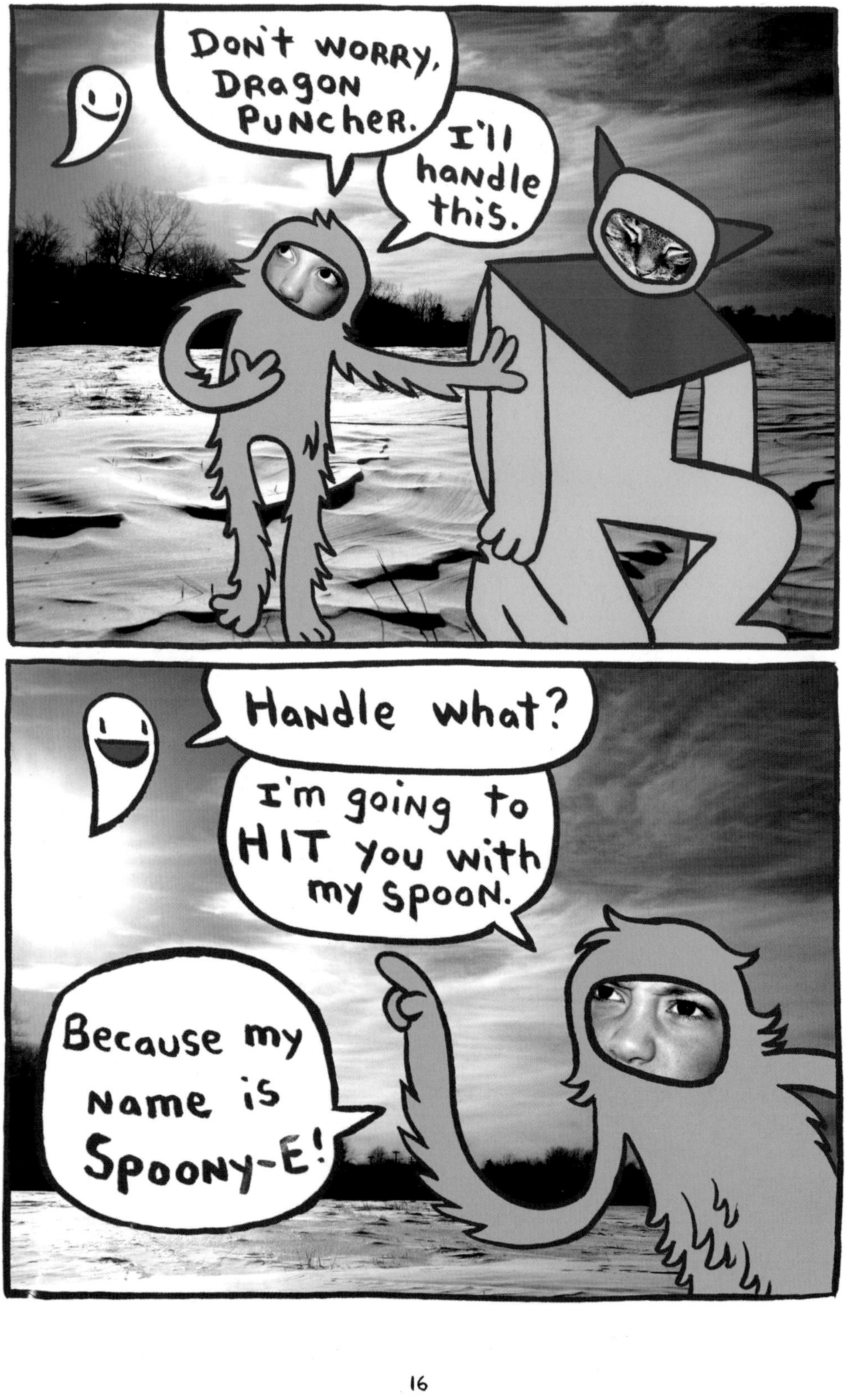
Don't worry, Dragon Puncher.
I'll handle this.
Handle what?
I'm going to HIT you with my spoon.
Because my name is Spoony-E!

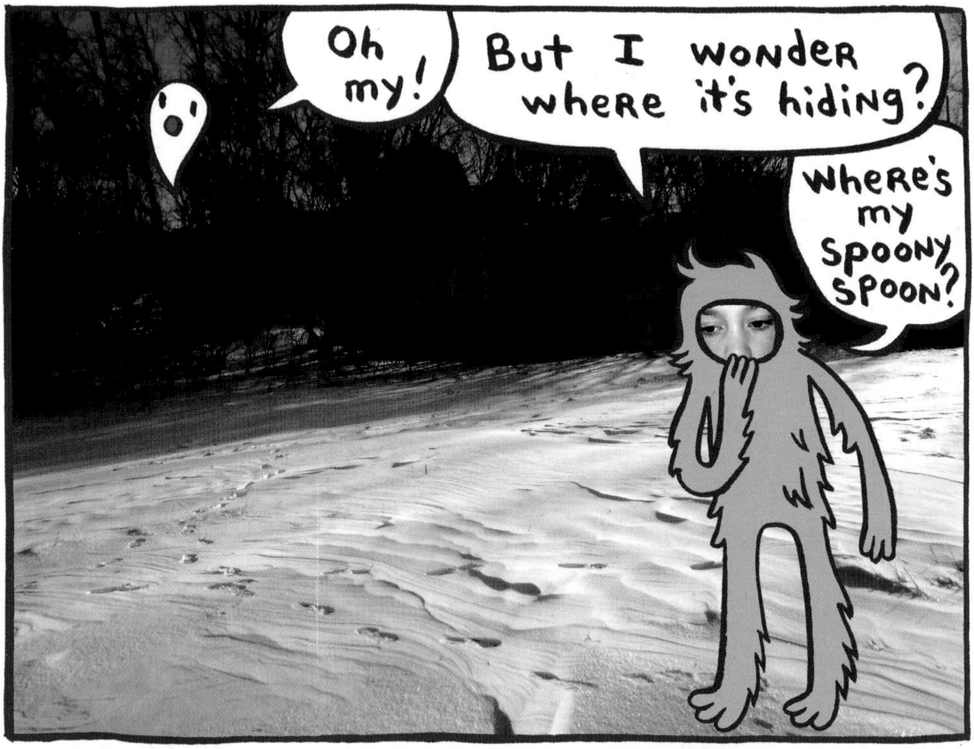
Oh my!
But I wonder where it's hiding?
Where's my spoony spoon?

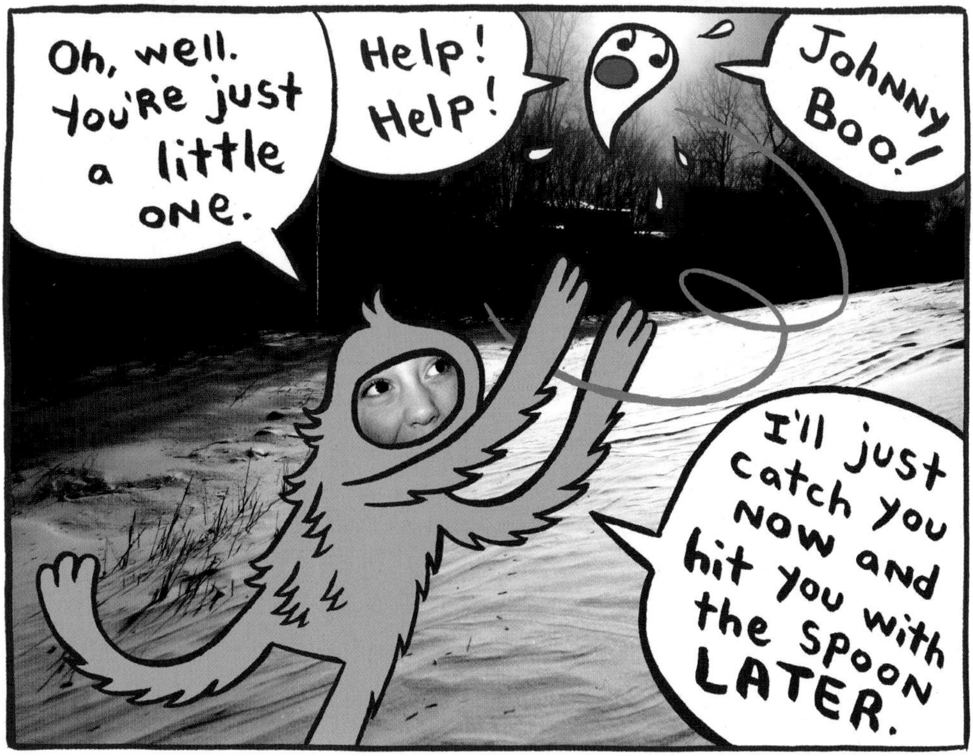
Oh, well. You're just a little one.
Help! Help!
Johnny Boo!
I'll just catch you now and hit you with the spoon LATER.

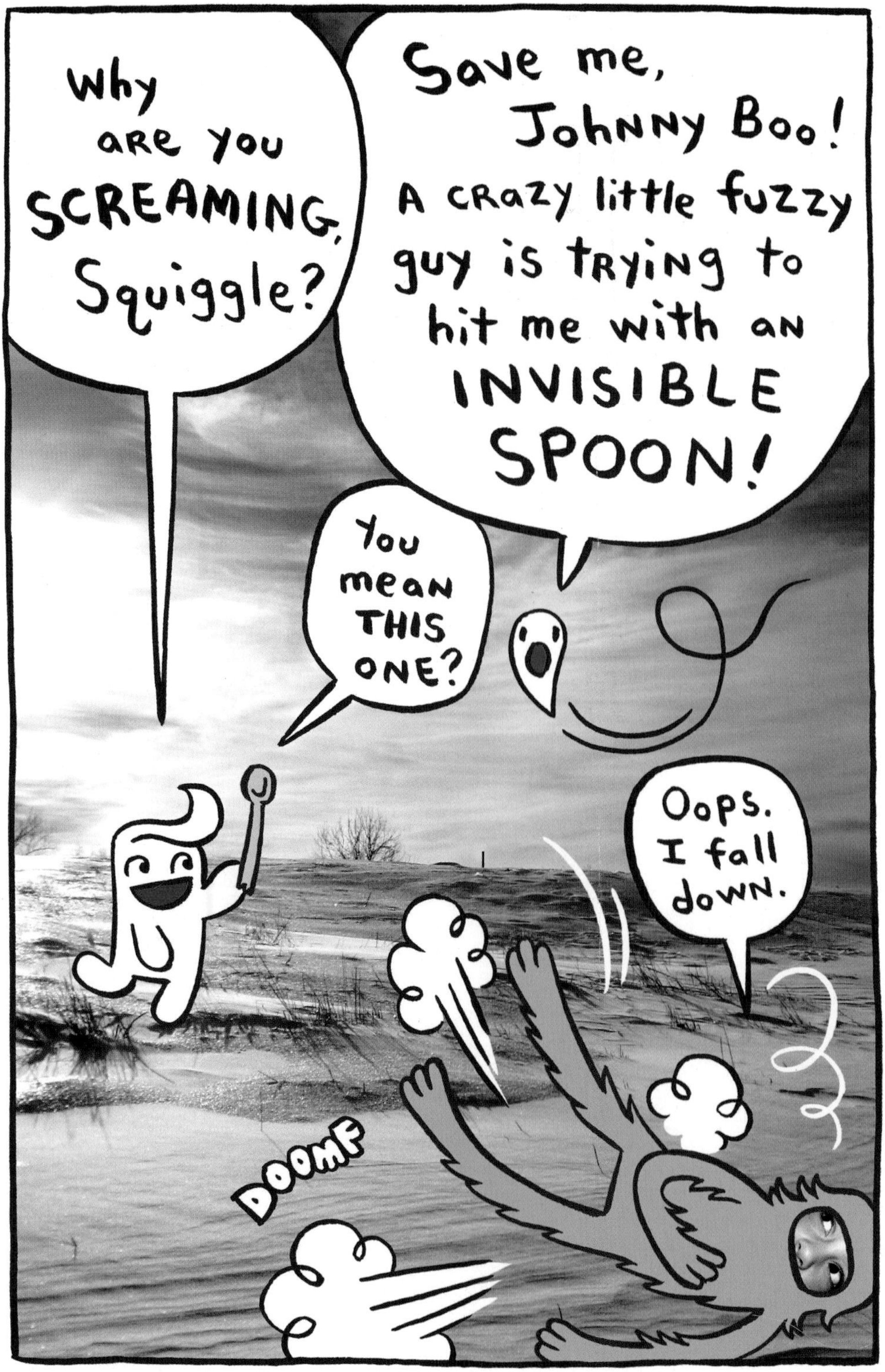
Why are you SCREAMING, Squiggle?
Save me, Johnny Boo! A crazy little fuzzy guy is trying to hit me with an INVISIBLE SPOON!
You mean THIS ONE?
Oops. I fall down.
DOOMF

CHAPTER FOUR:

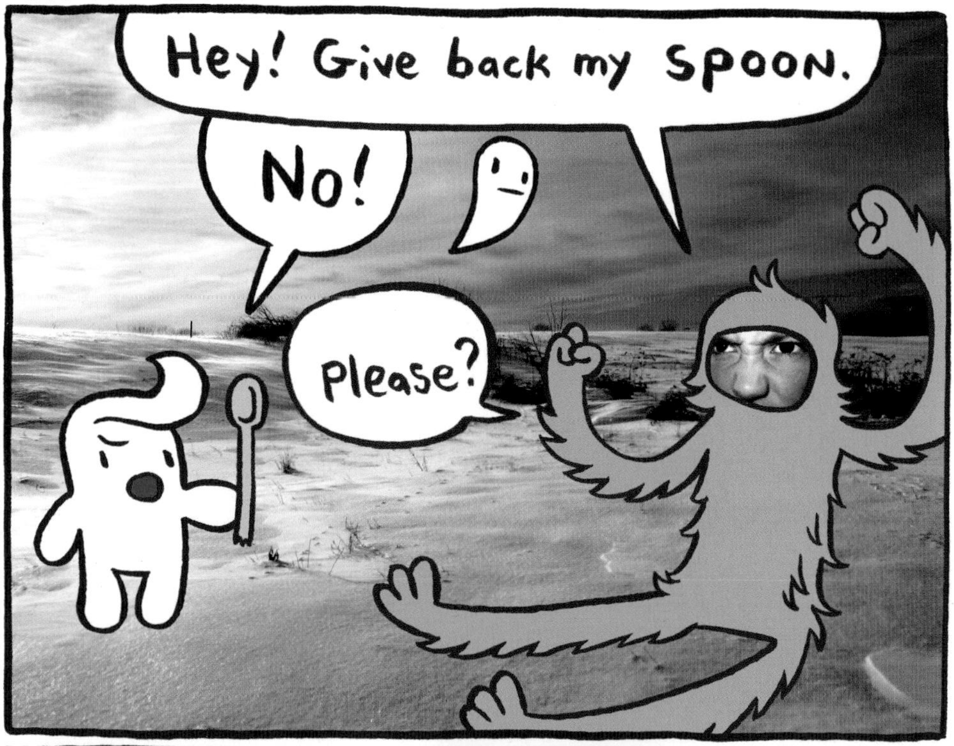
Hey! Give back my SPOON.
No!
Please?

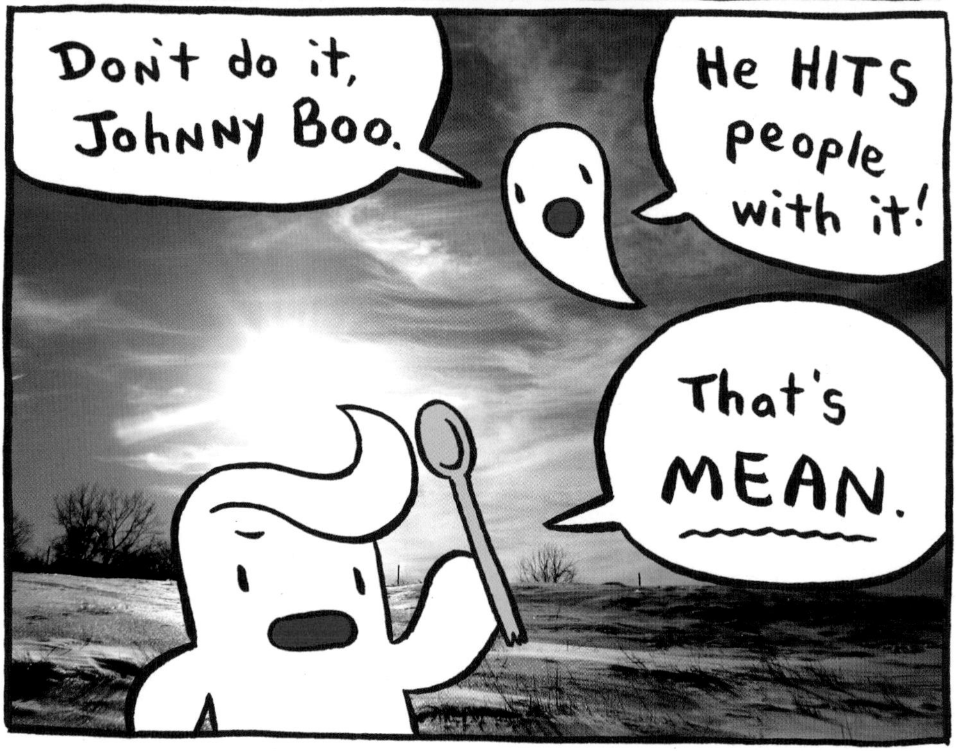
Don't do it, Johnny Boo.
He HITS people with it!
That's MEAN.

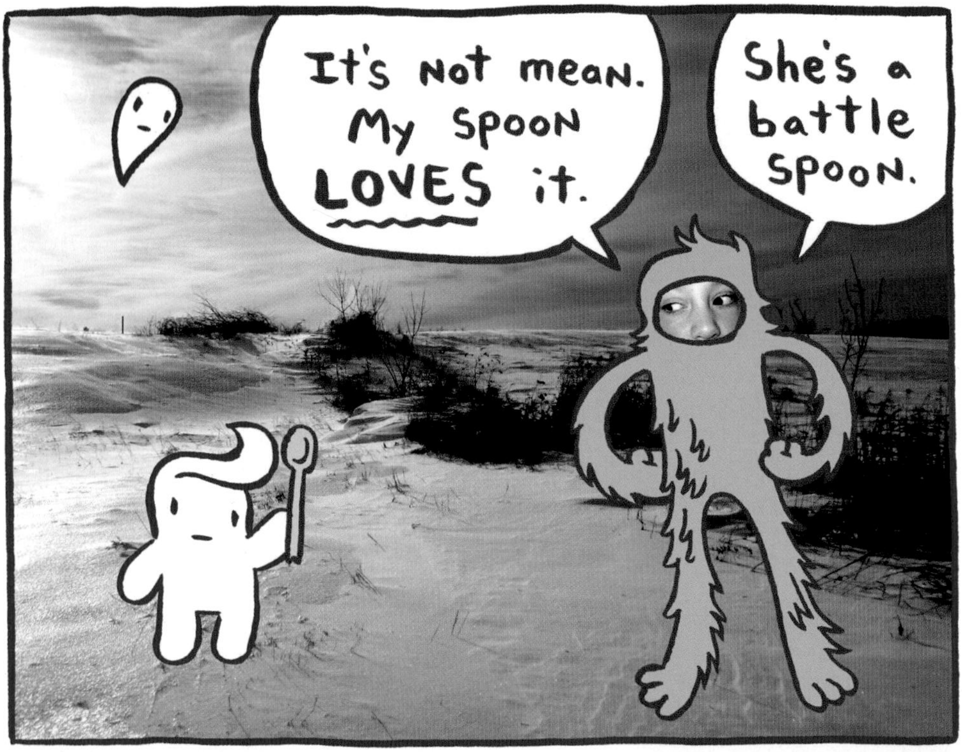
It's not mean. My spoon LOVES it.
She's a battle spoon.

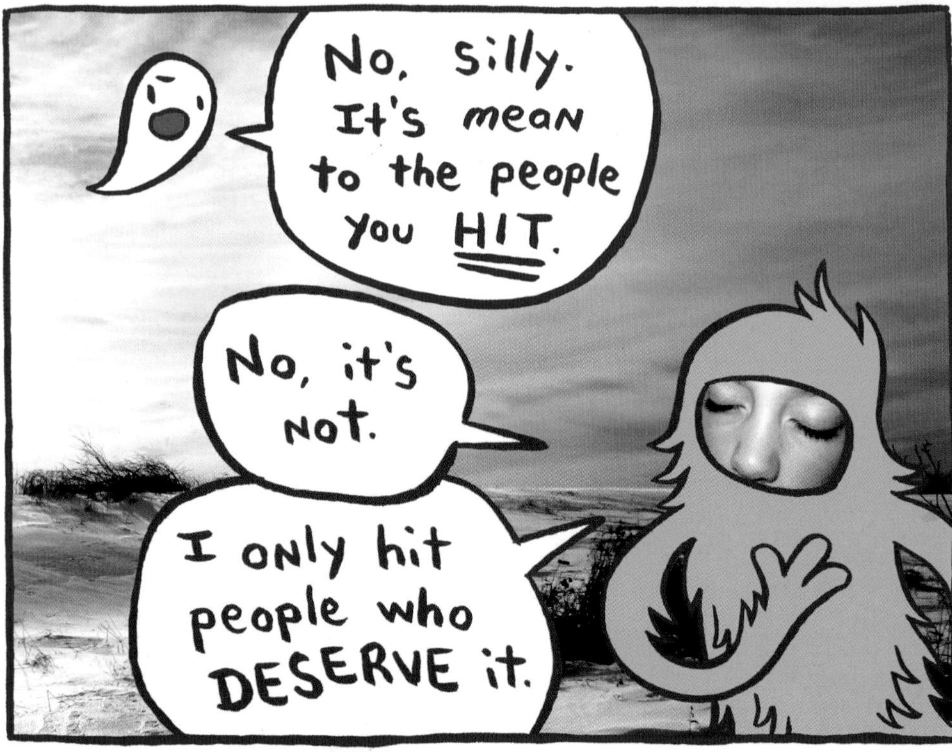
No, silly. It's mean to the people you HIT.
No, it's not.
I only hit people who DESERVE it.

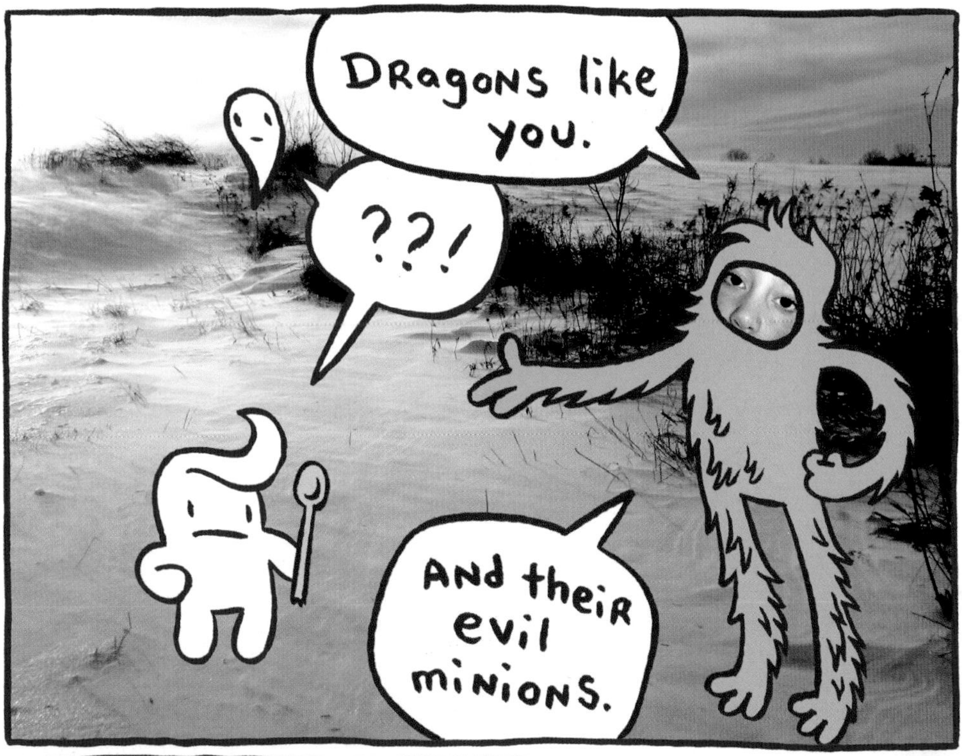
Dragons like you.
??!
And their evil minions.

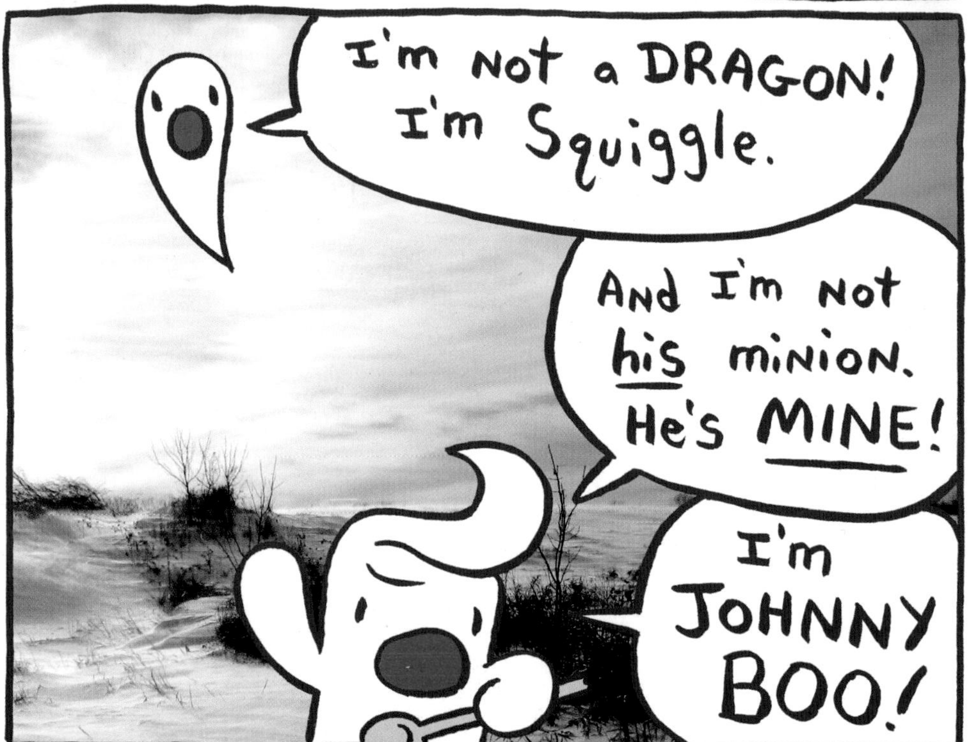
I'm not a DRAGON! I'm Squiggle.
And I'm not his minion. He's MINE!
I'm JOHNNY BOO!

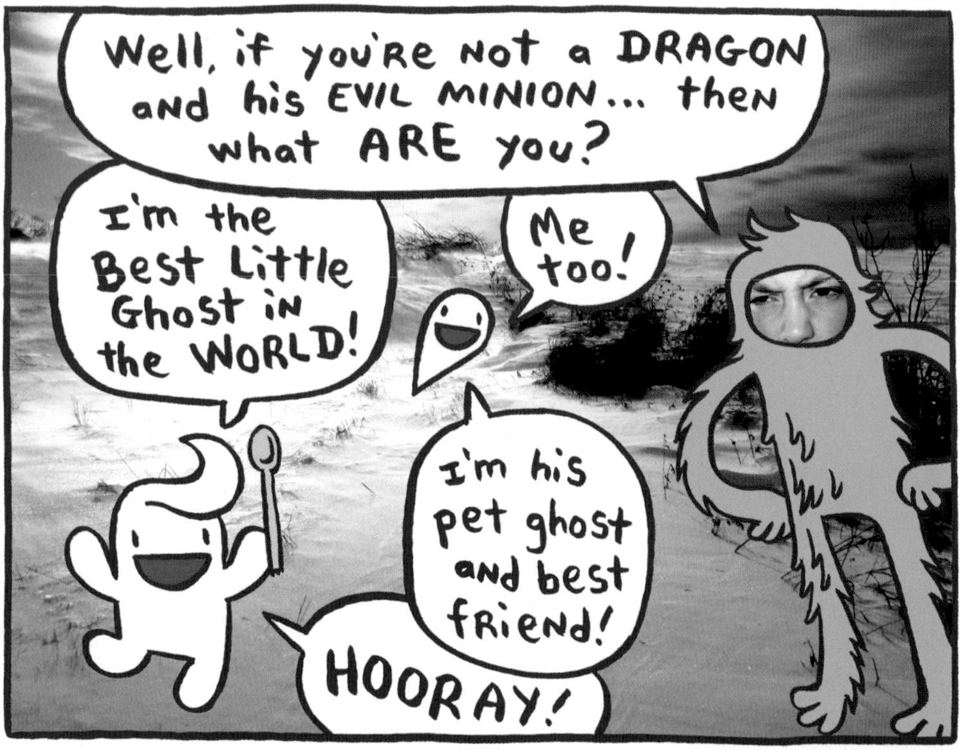
Well, if you're not a DRAGON and his EVIL MINION... then what ARE you?
I'm the Best Little Ghost in the WORLD!
Me too!
I'm his pet ghost and best friend!
HOORAY!

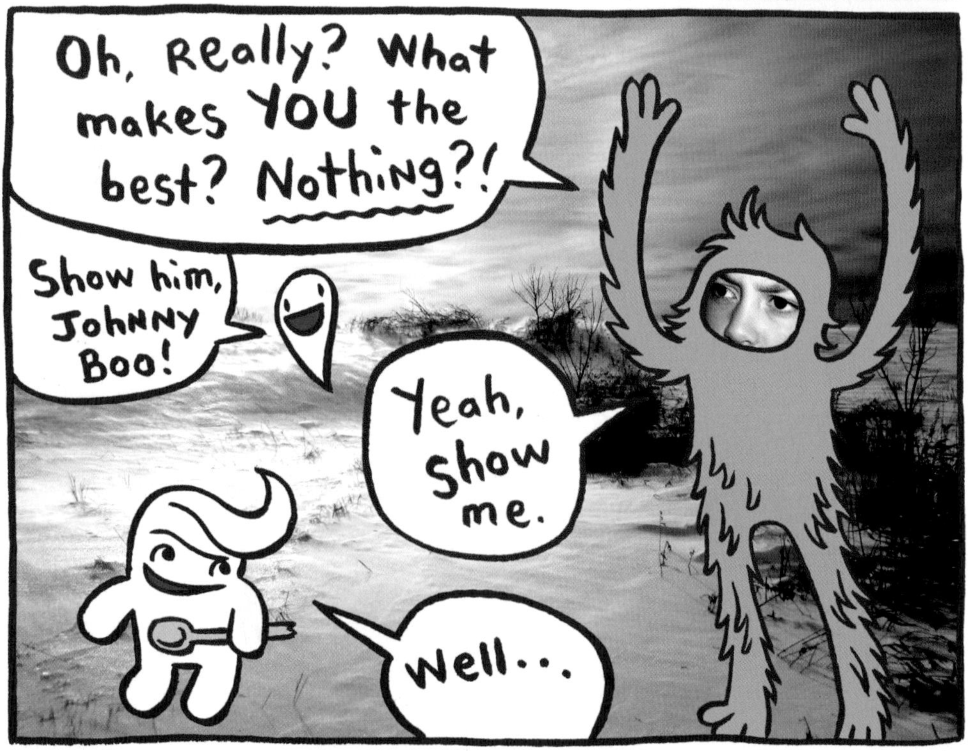
Oh, Really? What makes YOU the best? Nothing?!
Show him, Johnny Boo!
Yeah, Show me.
Well...

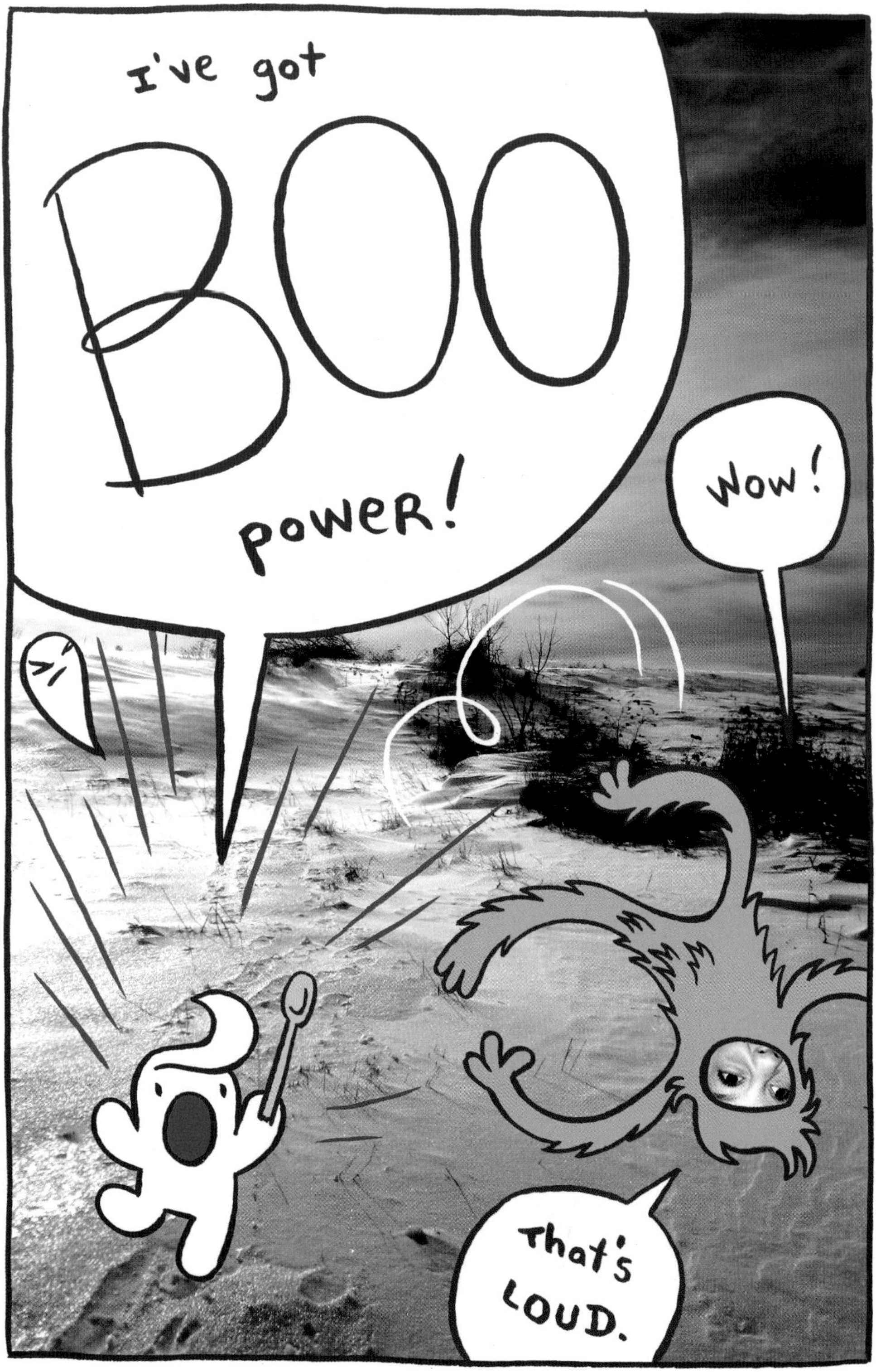
I've got BOO power!
Wow!
That's LOUD.

CHAPTER FIVE:

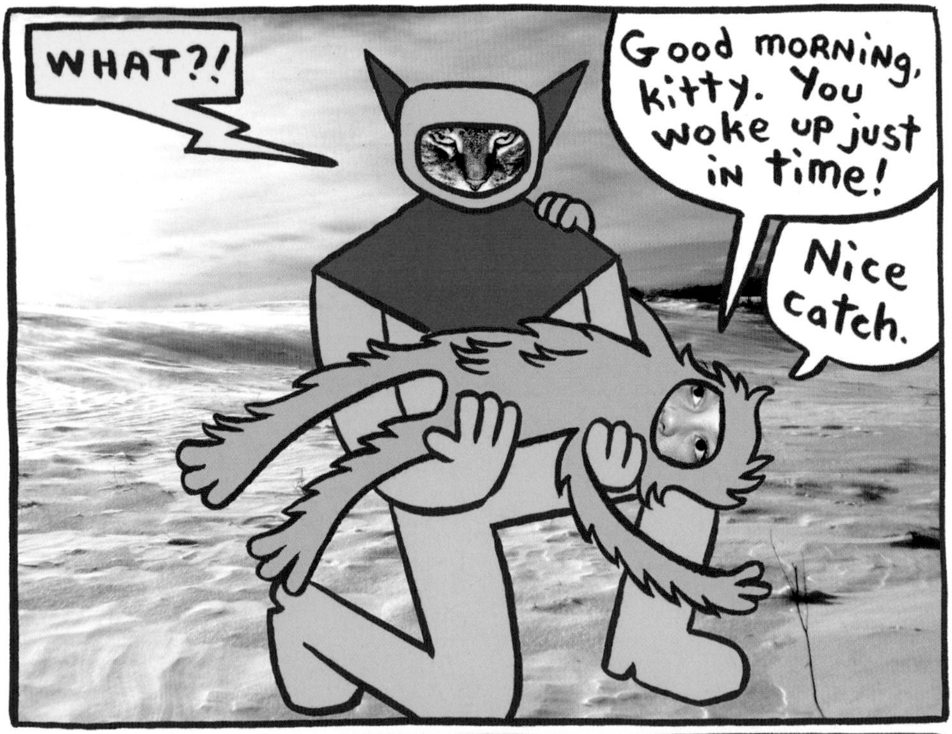
WHAT?!
Good morning, kitty. You woke up just in time!
Nice catch.

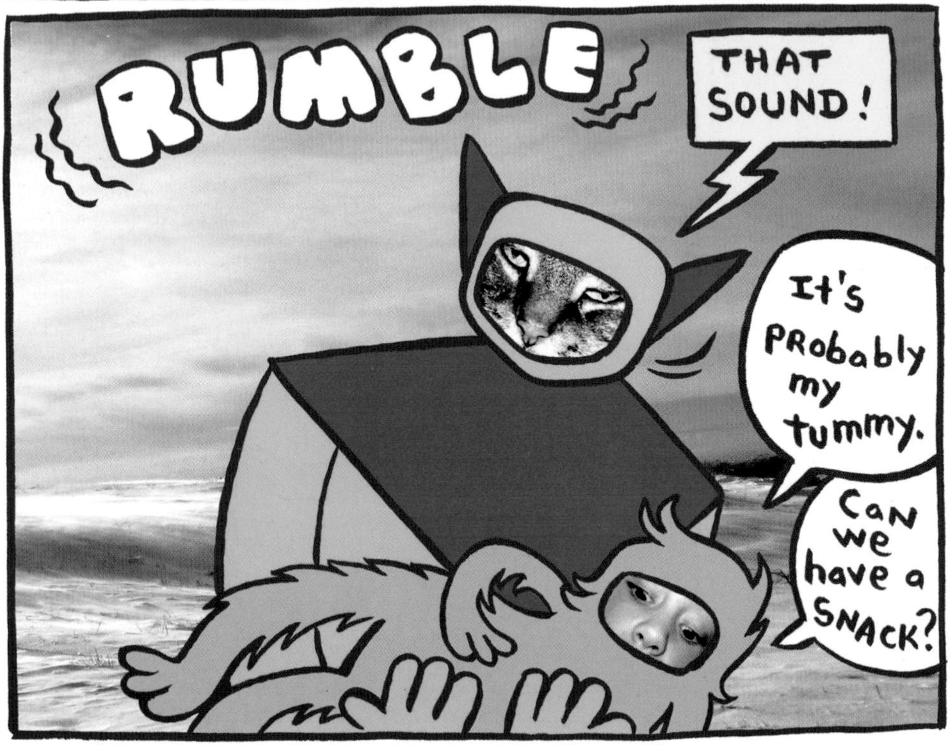
RUMBLE
THAT SOUND!
It's probably my tummy.
Can we have a SNACK?

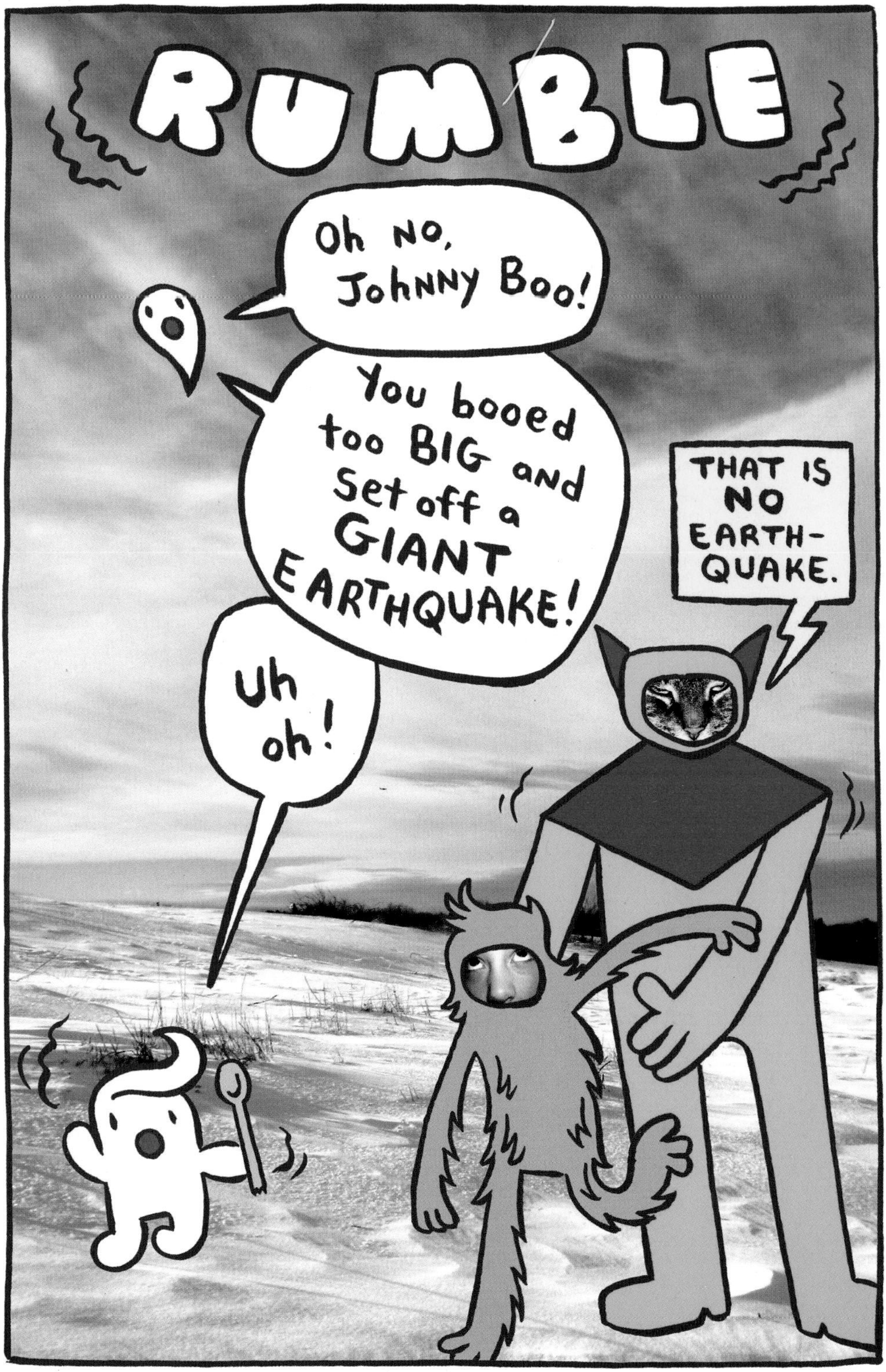
RUMBLE
Oh no, Johnny Boo!
You booed too BIG and set off a GIANT EARTHQUAKE!
Uh oh!
THAT IS NO EARTH-QUAKE.

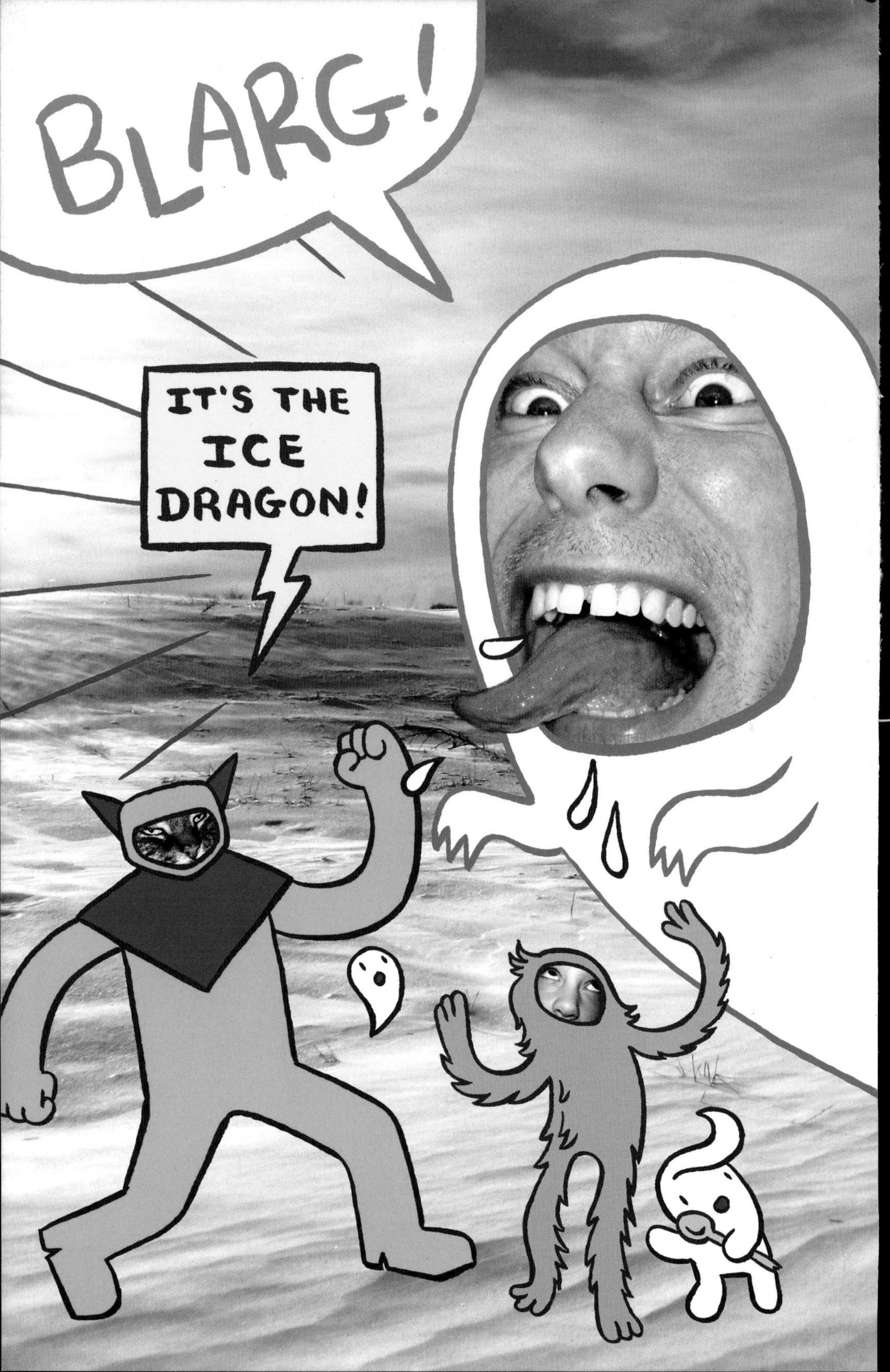
BLARG!
IT'S THE ICE DRAGON!

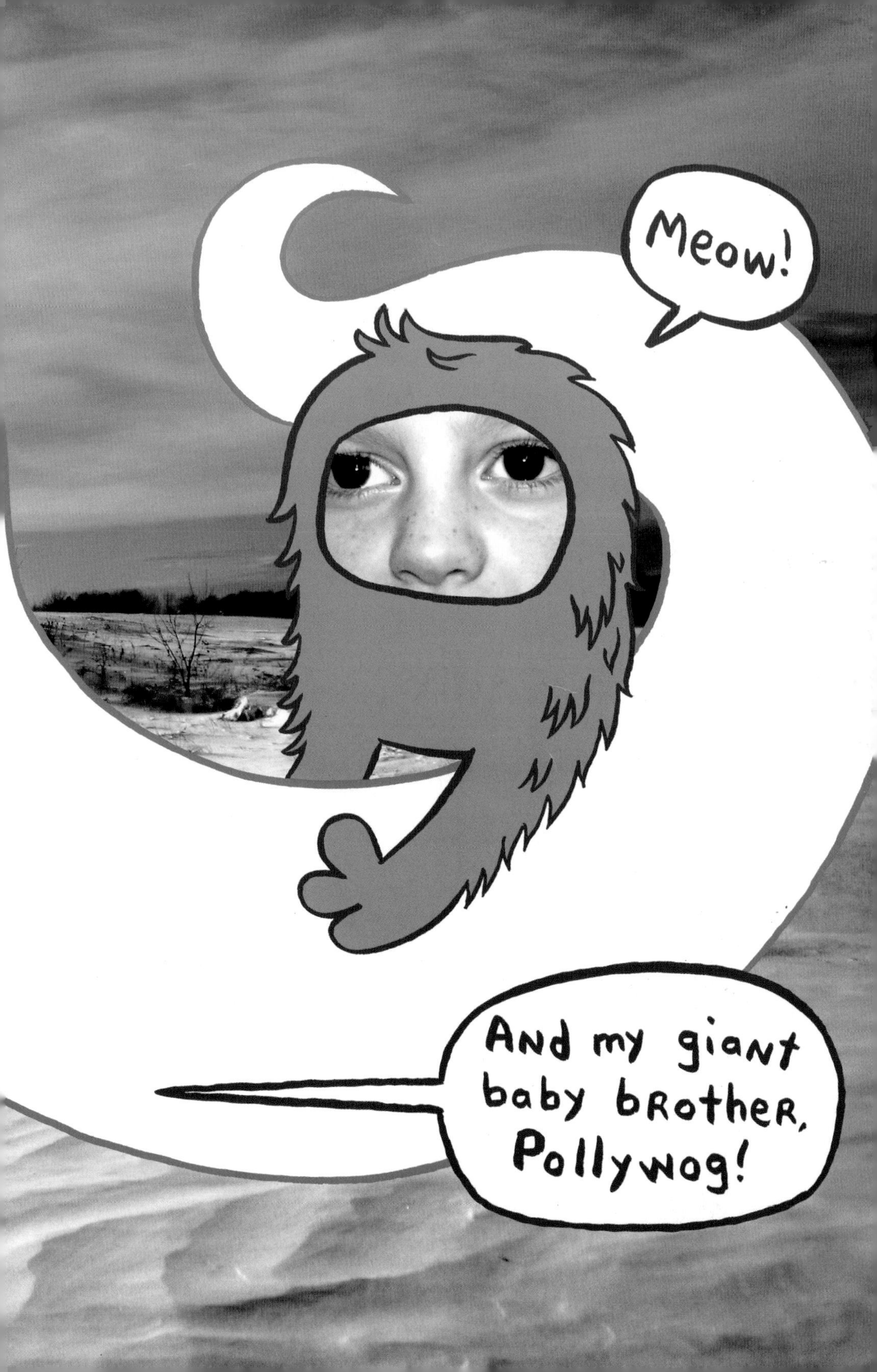
Meow!
And my giant baby brother, Pollywog!

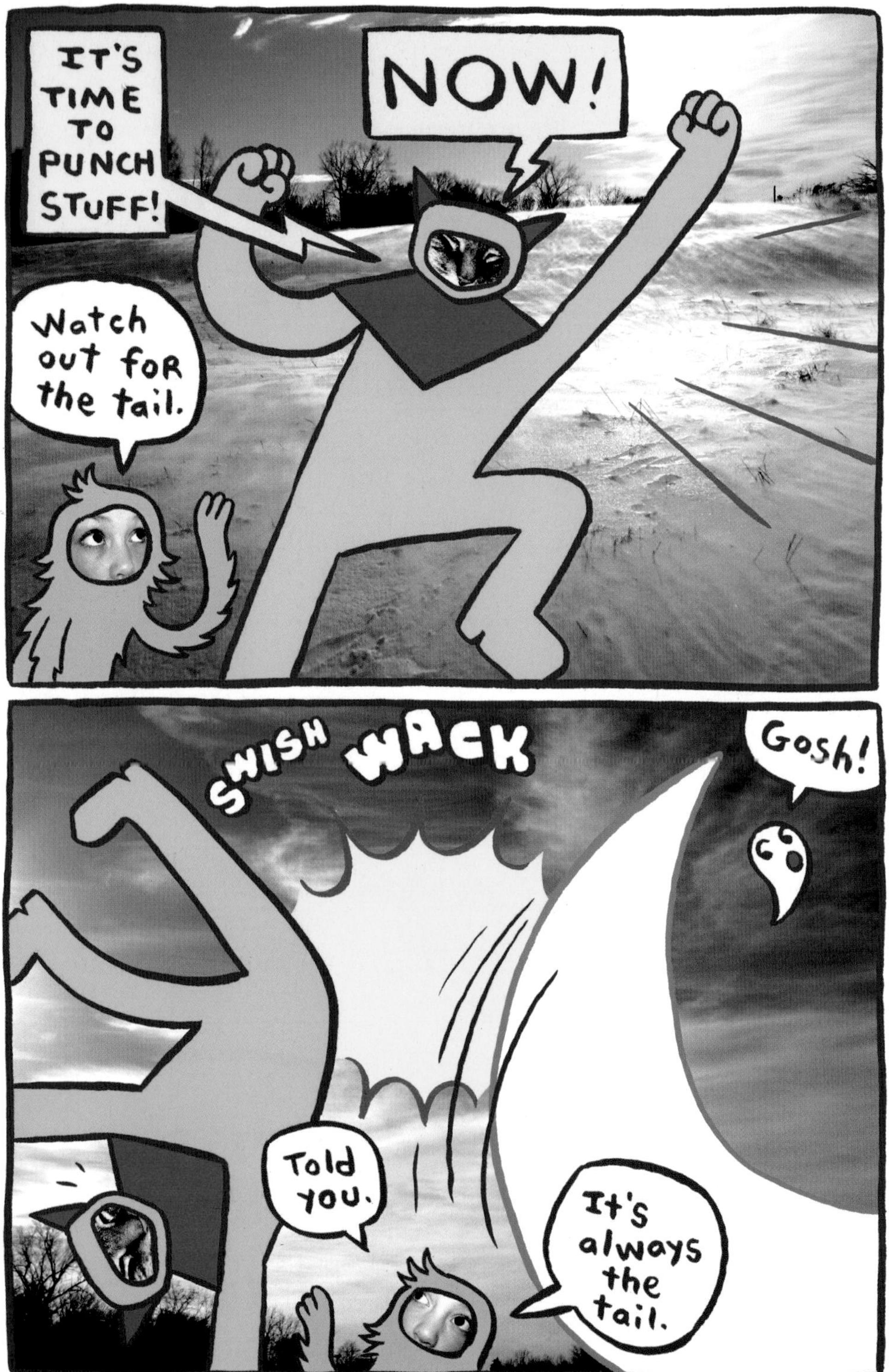
IT'S TIME TO PUNCH STUFF!
NOW!
Watch out for the tail.
SWISH
WACK
Gosh!
Told you.
It's always the tail.

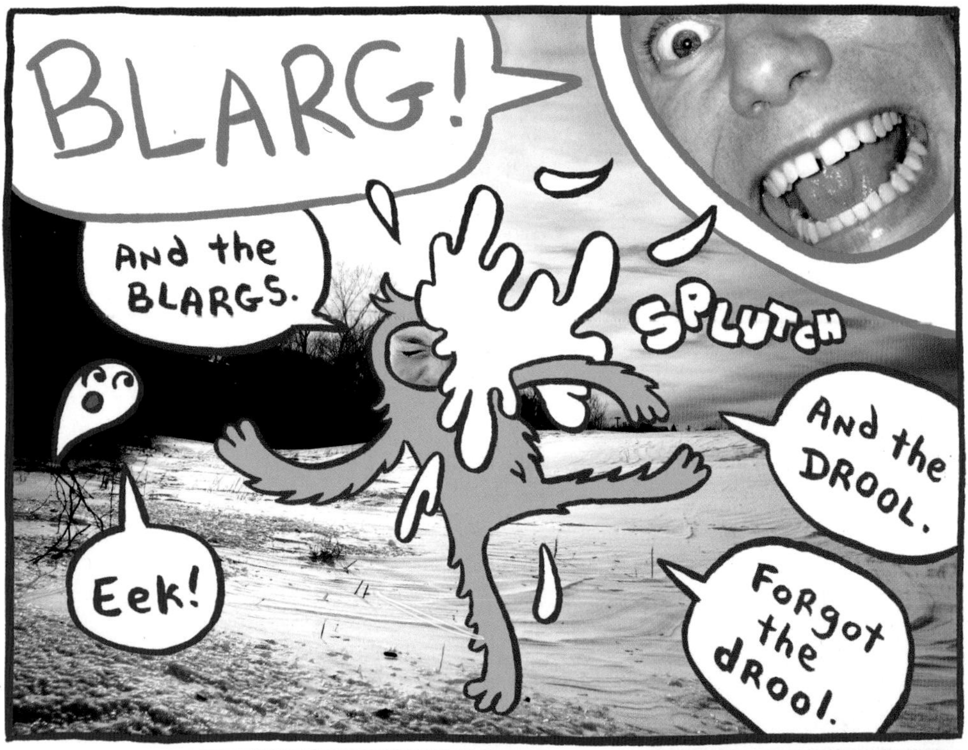
BLARG!
And the BLARGS.
SPLUTCH
And the DROOL.
Eek!
Forgot the drool.

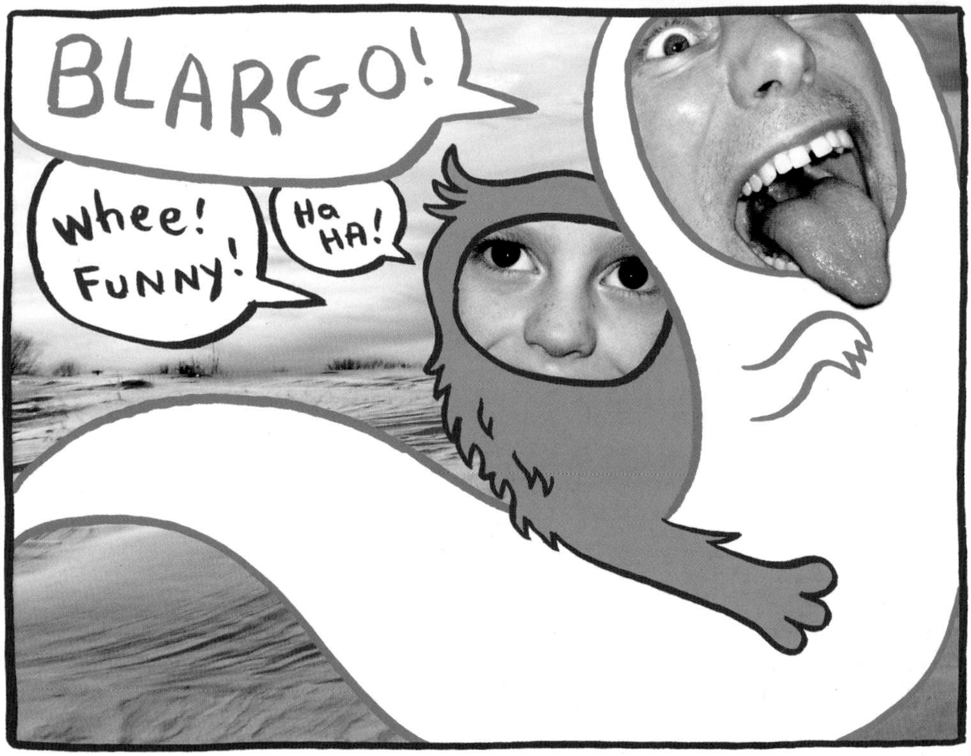
BLARGO!
whee! FUNNY!
Ha HA!

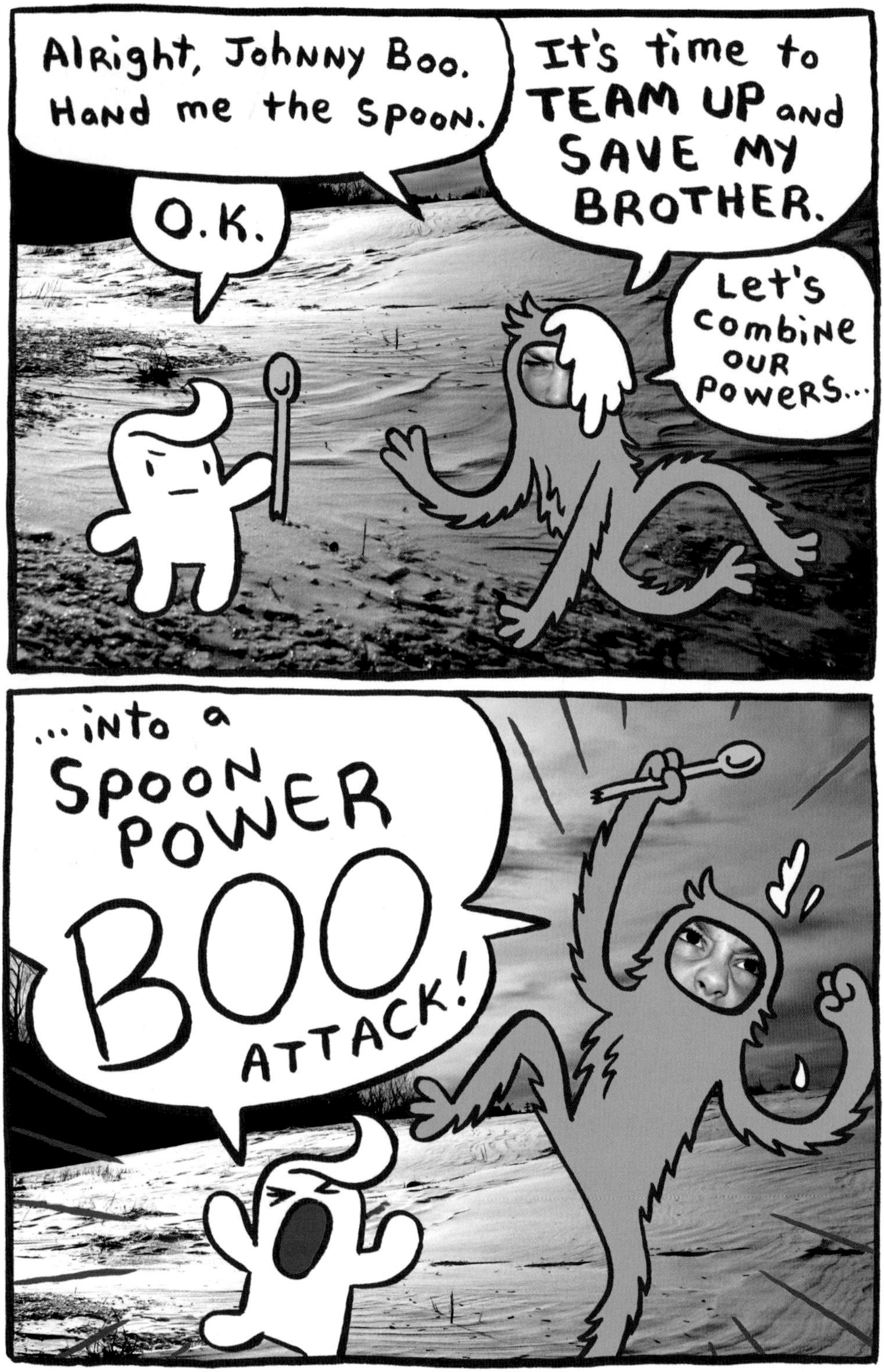

Alright, Johnny Boo. Hand me the spoon.
It's time to TEAM UP and SAVE MY BROTHER.
O.K.
Let's combine our powers...
...into a SPOON POWER BOO ATTACK!

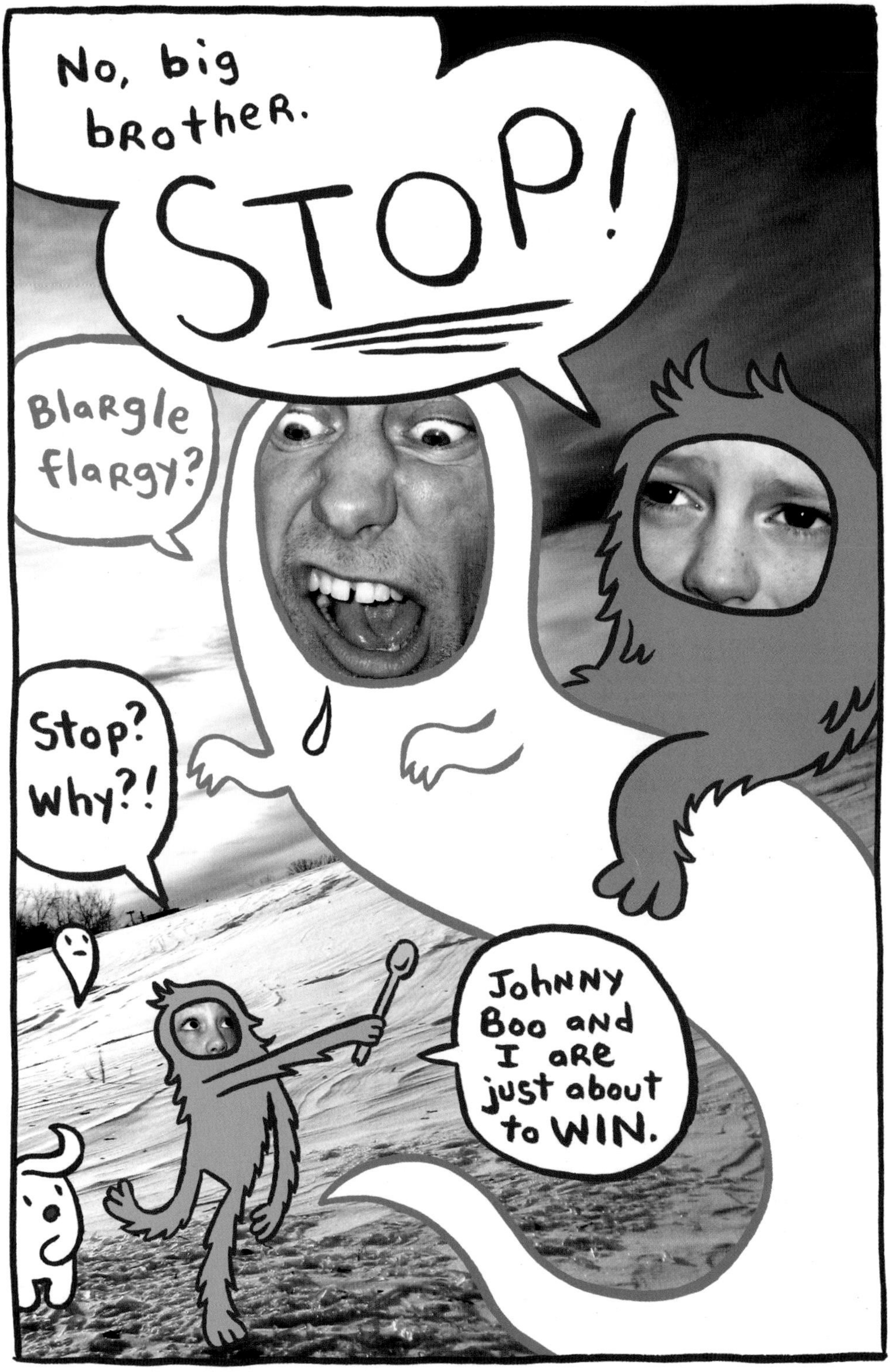
No, big brother.
STOP!
Blargle flargy?
Stop? Why?!
Johnny Boo and I are just about to WIN.

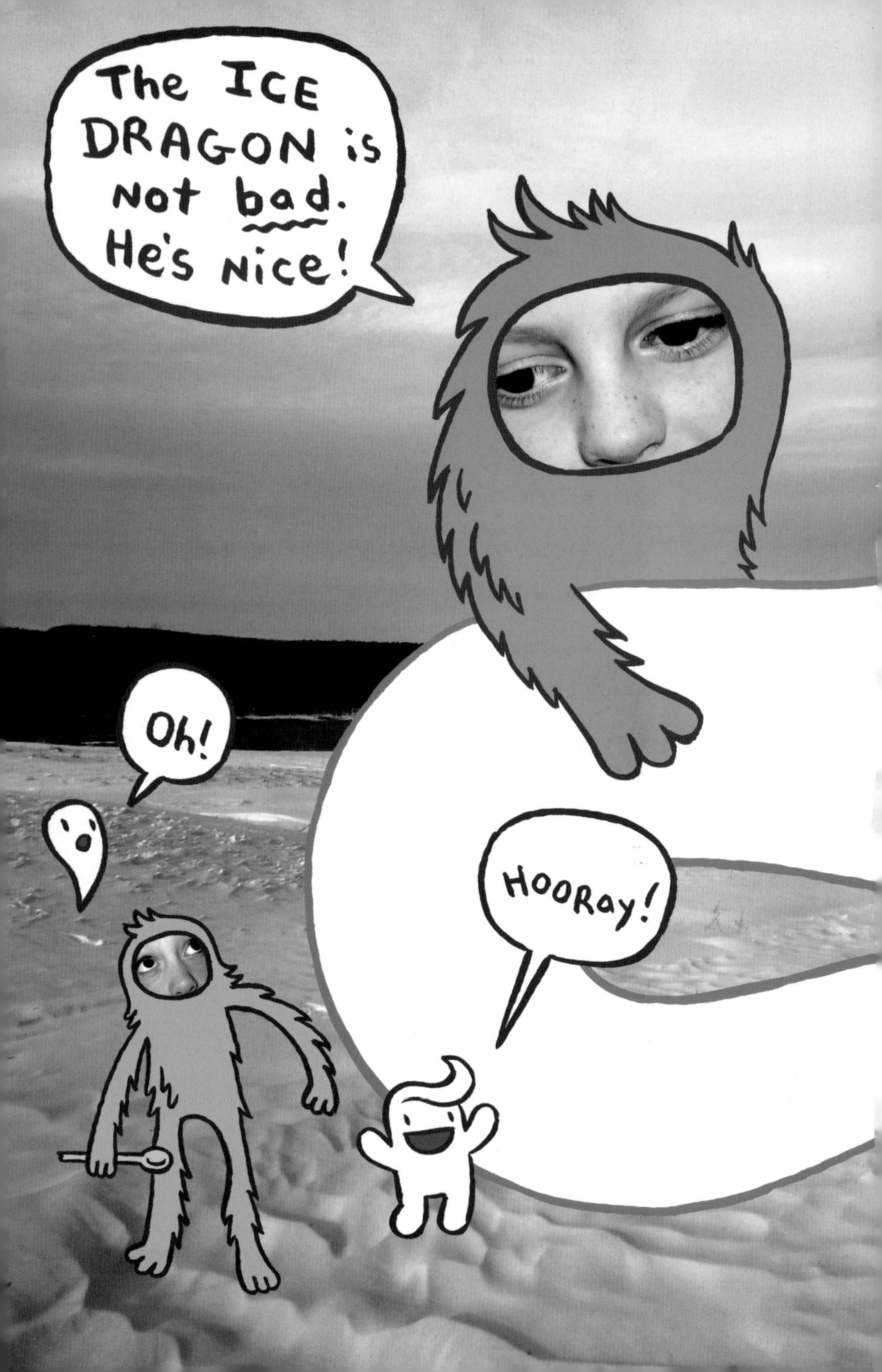
The ICE DRAGON is not bad. He's nice!
Oh!
HOORay!

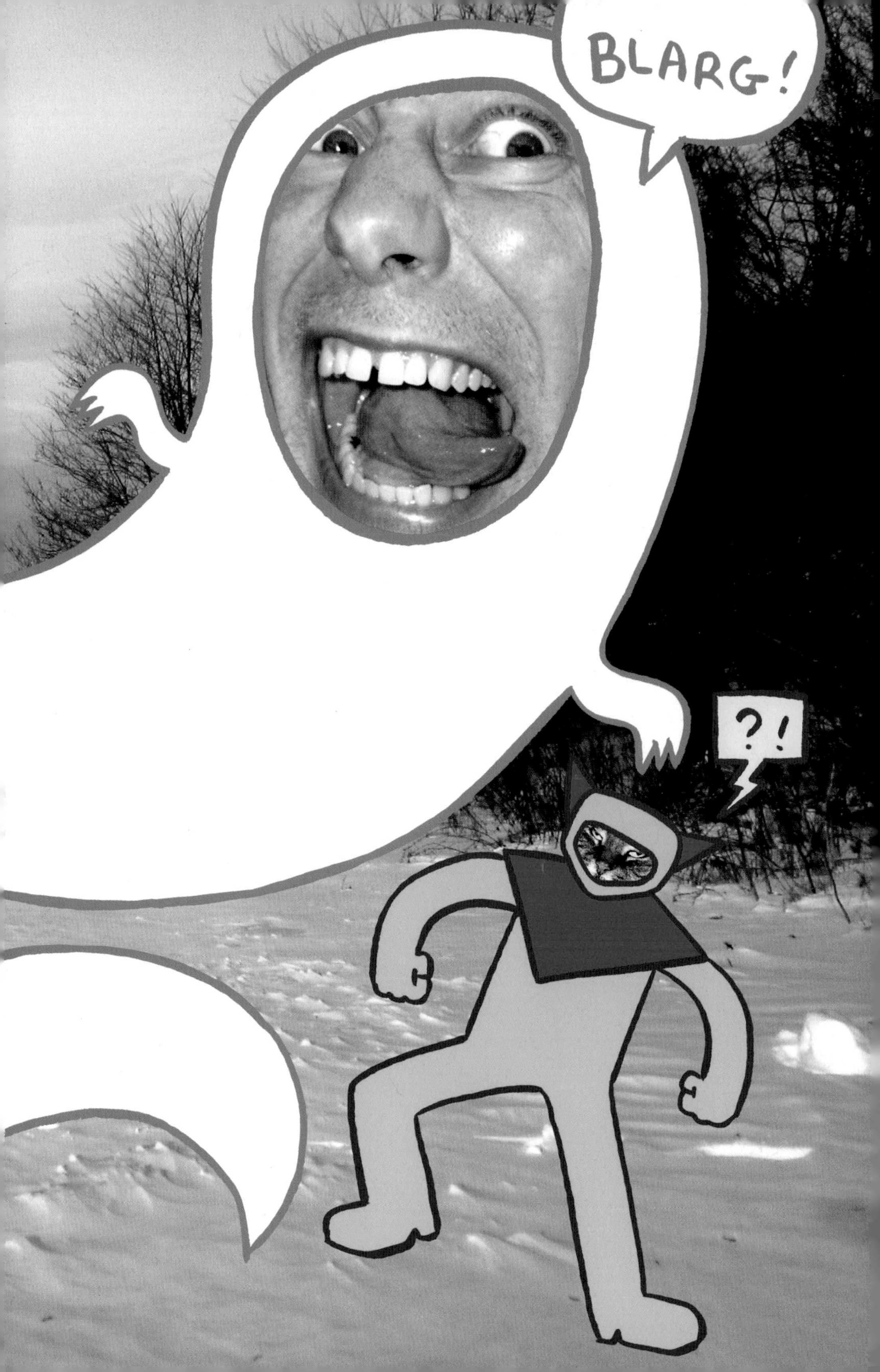
BLARG!
?!

CHAPTER SIX:

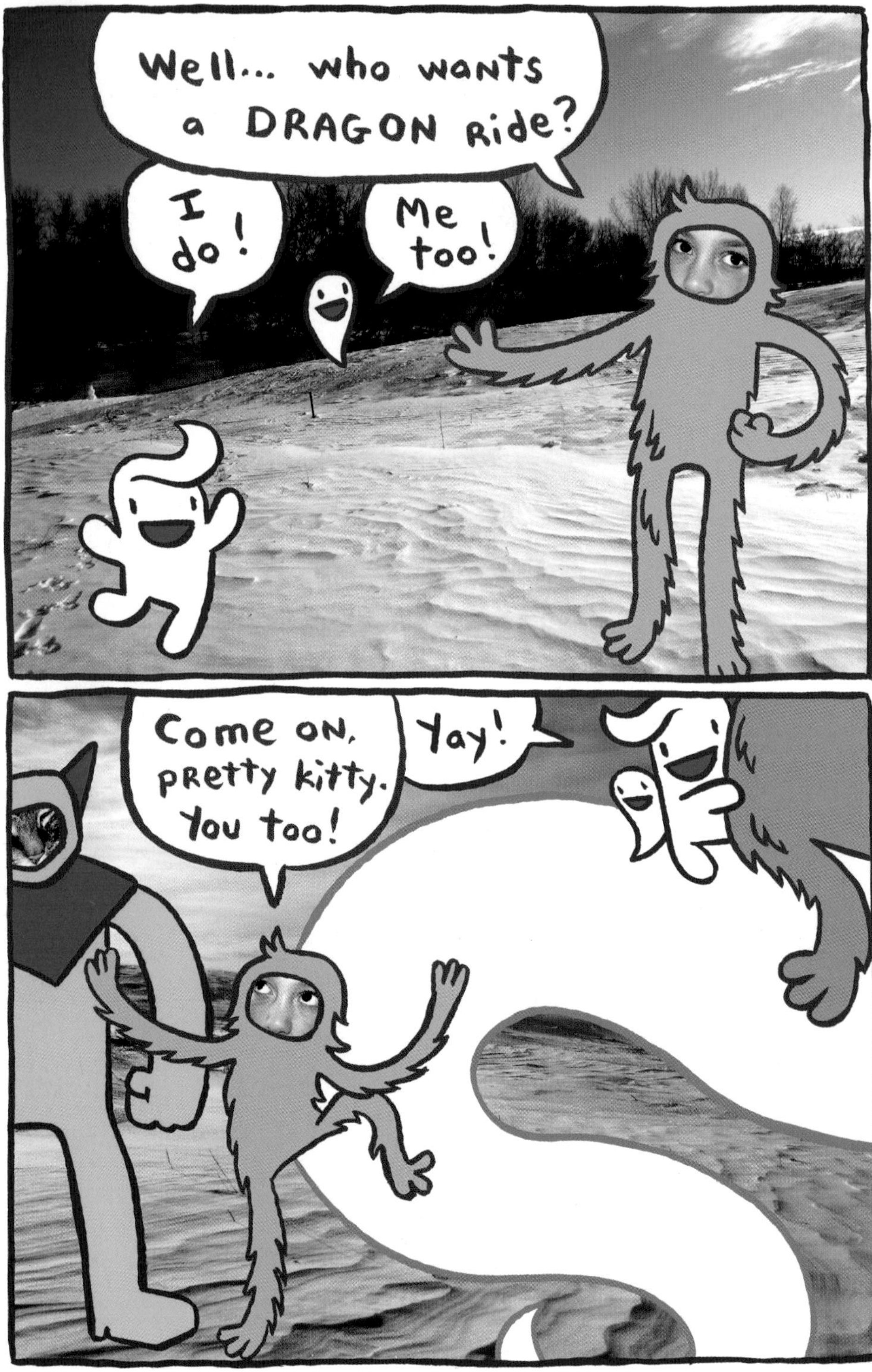
Well... who wants a DRAGON Ride?
I do!
Me too!
Come ON, pretty kitty. You too!
Yay!

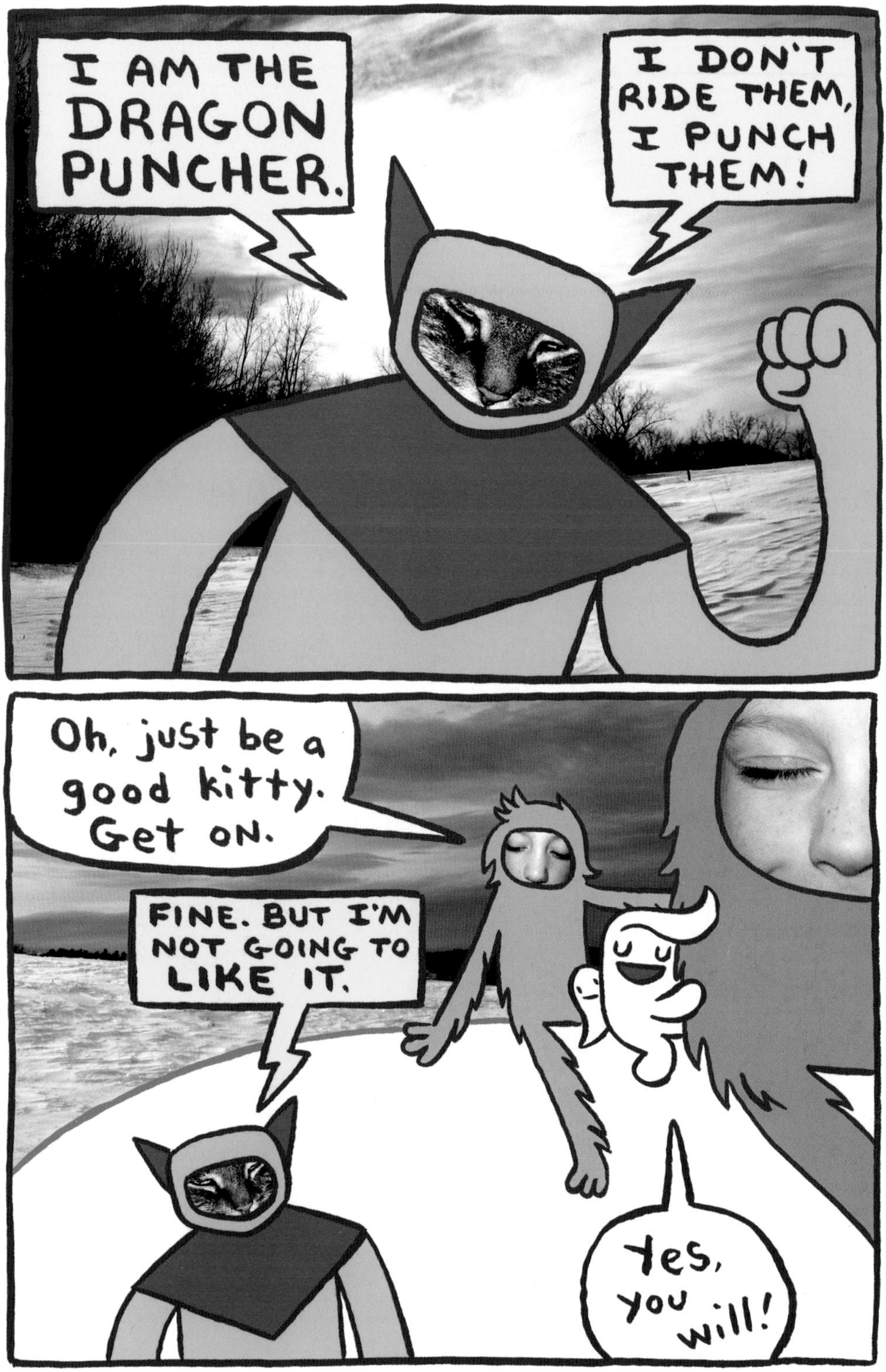
I AM THE DRAGON PUNCHER.
I DON'T RIDE THEM, I PUNCH THEM!
Oh, just be a good kitty. Get on.
FINE. BUT I'M NOT GOING TO LIKE IT.
Yes, you will!

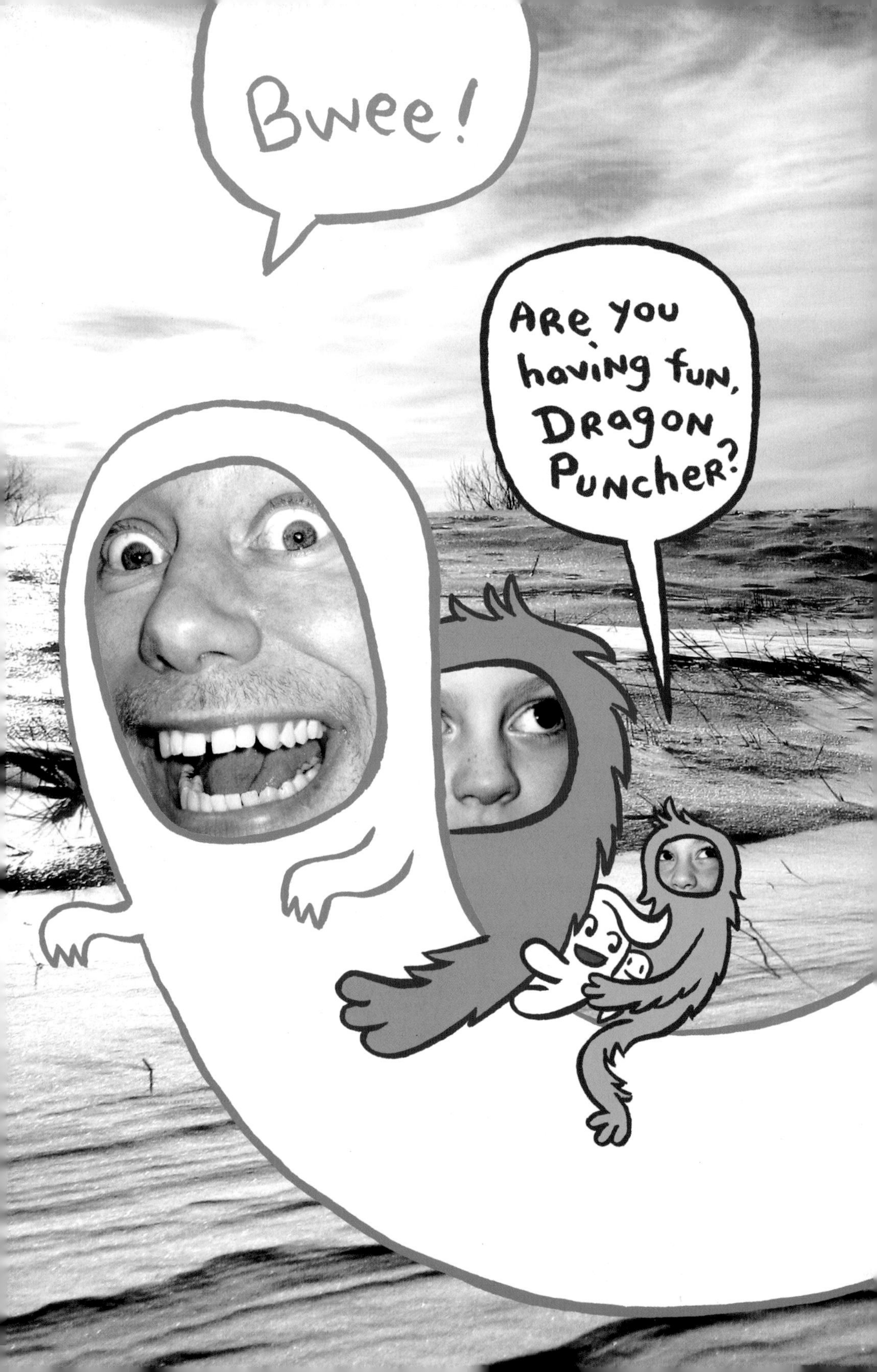
Bwee!
Are you having fun, Dragon Puncher?

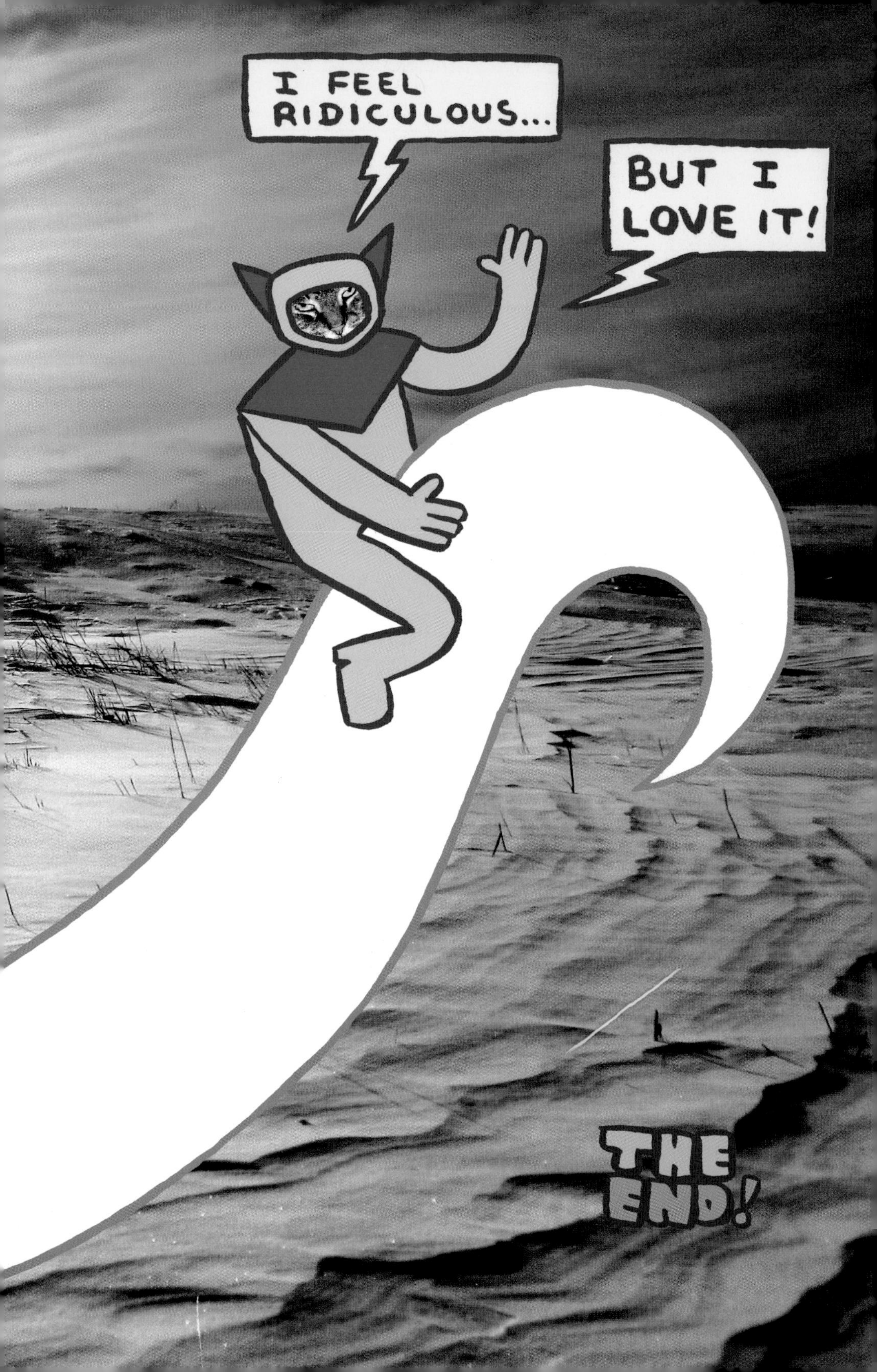
I FEEL RIDICULOUS...
BUT I LOVE IT!
THE END!

STARRING

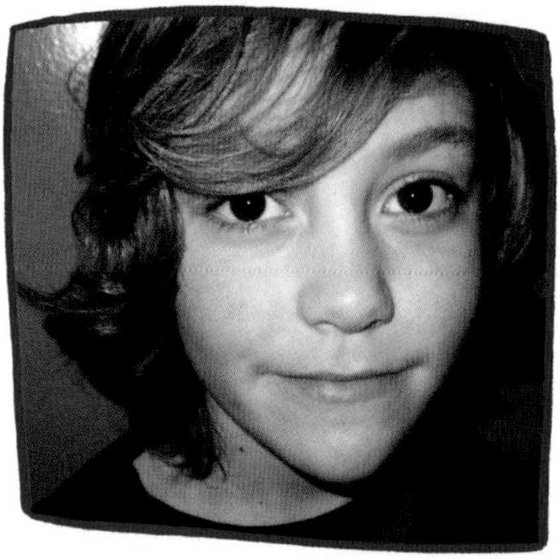

ELI KOCHALKA (AGE 10) AS SPOONY-E.

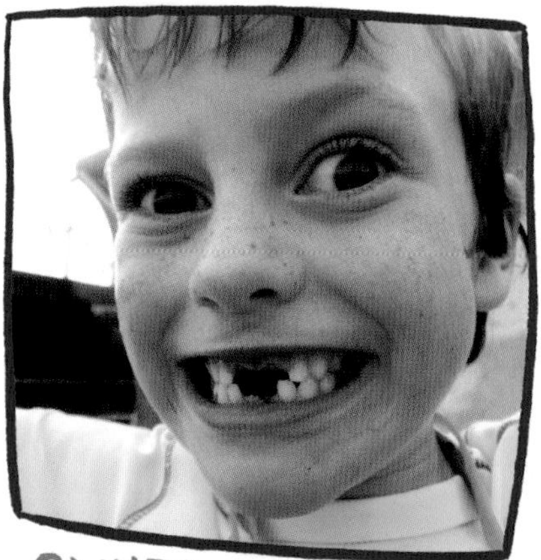

OLIVER KOCHALKA (AGE 6) AS POLLYWOG.

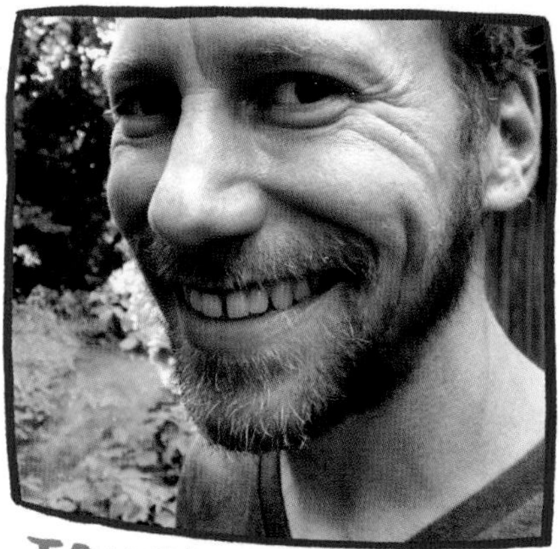

JAMES KOCHALKA (AGE 47) AS THE ICE DRAGON.

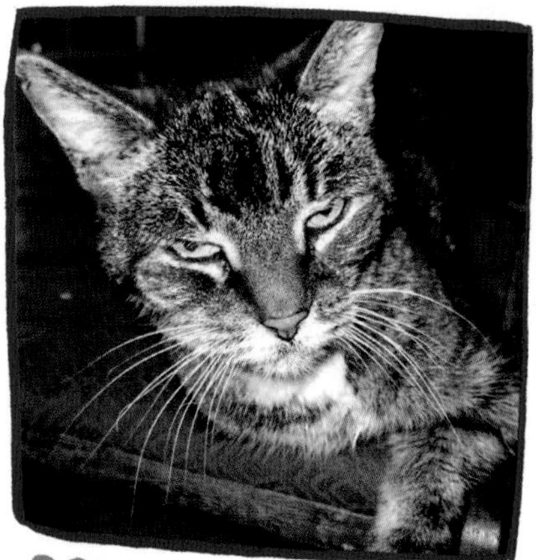

SPANDY THE CAT (AGE 19) AS THE DRAGON PUNCHER.

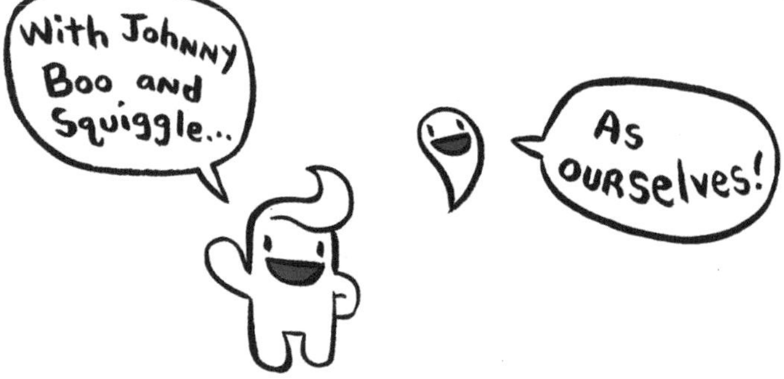
With Johnny Boo and Squiggle...
As ourselves!

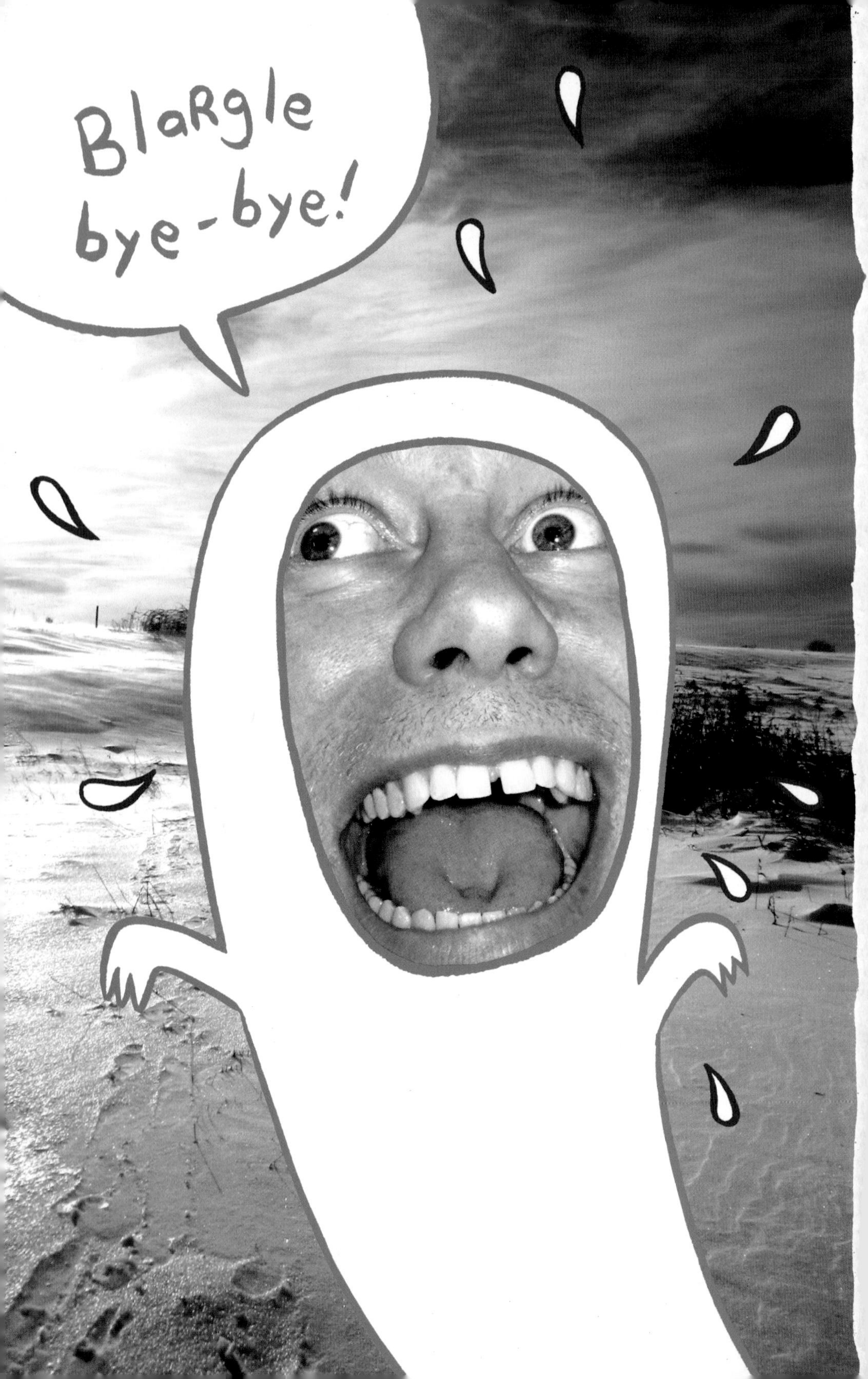
Blargle bye-bye!